The Last Resort

A Novel

Kay Tobler Liss

The Last Resort

A Novel

Kay Tobler Liss

Plain View Press
1101 W. 34th Street, STE 404

http://plainviewpress.net
Austin, TX 78705

Copyright © 2020 Kay Tobler Liss. All rights reserved under International and Pan-American Copyright Conventions. No part of this book may be reproduced or distributed in any form or by any means, or stored in a data base or retrieval system, without written permission from the author. All rights, including electronic, are reserved by the author and publisher.

ISBN: 978-1-63210-080-1
ebook ISBN: 978-1-63210-081-8
Library of Congress Control Number: 2020934180

Cover photo by Kay Tobler Liss
Cover Design by Pam Knight

Chapters "The Surf" and "Tearing Away the Veil" from *The Last Resort,* in slighty different form, were included in the anthology *On Montauk: A Literary Celebration*, edited by Celine Keating and Ed Johann, 2016.
Excerpts from *The Dream of the Earth* by Thomas Berry, published by Sierra Club Books, 1988, are reprinted with permission from Counterpoint.

This is a work of fiction. With the exception of some known historical events and figures, all characters, places, incidents, and dialogues are a product of the author's imagination or are used fictitiously, and any resemblance to actual persons, living or dead, is entirely coincidental.

*To my father, George Tobler,
who inspired the first version of this story,
and to the Indigenous Peoples of the world*

White Line

I'm rushing into the tunnel light, leaving everything behind. I try not to think, just keep my mind on the white line ahead, let it lead me, take me as far as it goes. There's nothing else now, a thought as chilling as it is strangely thrilling. A feeling like ice fighting fire runs through my veins.

But no more thoughts. Follow the white line. I glance at the speedometer: pushing into the red zone. I loosen my grip, so hard, on the wheel and ease up my foot from the floor.

Finally out of the tunnel and heading due east. The city's jagged gray outline—once appearing to me so promising in its bold thrusting upward—now seems like a sad, worn scar upon the edge of the horizon, fading, enveloped in a surreal haze of sunset and smog.

A little less frantic than moments ago, but I'm still too close to spinning out of control. I take some deep breaths and wish I could shut off my mind for a while. Why is it so hard to possess such a power? Maybe if I'd taken Barry's advice—how many years ago?—back in the late '60s, and learned TM, I could clear my mind at will.

Yet, if I had taken his advice, the entire course of my life might have been different, and at this moment in time I wouldn't be here on the Long Island Expressway, going this killing speed in my car, in my mind.

I better slow down. The wheel's shaking in my hands. I glance in the rearview mirror. Normally so implacably calm, it's a face I almost don't recognize, every muscle so taut, eyes wide and wild, like some crazed character conjured up in a bad dream.

I refocus my eyes intently ahead, try to imagine myself like Barry, serenely meditating on a mountaintop in India. It's strange how, even in extreme moments like this, when things can't get much worse and someone else's life appears infinitely better, it's hard to put myself in another's life. I am who I am—and who I will be?

Who I will be, who I will be. Suddenly my thoughts retreat to that distant, idyllic time as a freshman in college, studying the Greek classics. My life stretching brightly ahead down an uncluttered road, how terrifying to me was the ancient Greek concept of fate: that chorus like a chill wind blowing ceaselessly through the plays, whispering of a character's sad but sure destiny, despite how young and full of promise he was.

I must stop letting my mind wander so far! Just focus on the straight, white line ahead. How purposeful and clear it is, like my life … but … but isn't that turning out to be no longer true, and maybe was always more an illusion, something I constructed, one comforting lie upon another?

My grip gets tighter on the wheel again, my foot presses closer to the floor. How easily it responds, how intoxicating the rush feels.

Yes, there it is! I started out wanting to do something good, nothing too grand. I saw that shining line between the just and the unjust, but then that clear line began to disappear: lawyers and the corporations we represent, just wanting to win, no matter what. And in a time when people judge you more by how much money you make, if you win at whatever you do, or how much power you wield, speaking of what is good and honorable sounds oddly quaint and anachronistic.

Still, in spite of the growing grimness I felt in my work—the sleazy deals and plea bargains, corrupt judges and defense of those I knew were pre-eminently guilty—I probably could have persevered, if it hadn't been for …

Red zone, definitely crash and burn time if I think about her. Steady now, focus on the white line again. See how it leads into the darkness spreading out wider and wider the farther I look? Like my life, starting out at a fixed point then breaking up into indefinable fragments disappearing into a fathomless black hole. An end, no doubt—but could it also be a beginning?

Enough, enough thinking!

I'll just keep going as far as I can go. There're hardly any other cars now. I'm getting out into the country, the moon and stars shining brightly overhead. The air is tinged with a saltiness, and there're no sounds in my head but the whirring of wheels spinning on pavement.

Past Amagansett

I'm nearing the end of the island now. Through the bright moonlight, I see outlines of palatial homes tucked behind lofty elms and perfect lawns. Now they're disappearing dramatically from view and I'm suddenly thrust out onto a desolate stretch of sand, the ocean's roar beyond the line of dunes getting closer as the wind whips sand gustily across the road. Human time recedes as earth time—the sea, sand and wind—swirls to the foreground. The incongruous lights of a lone motel beckon meekly off in the distance. Telephone poles lean wearily against the sky, humbled by the constant onslaught of the wind.

We would rarely venture out this far during our summer sojourns to the Hamptons. Going past Amagansett and our neat compound of beach cottages was somehow like dropping off the edge of the world. How metaphorically fitting I should be here now.

As I leave the flat, straight stretch of sand, I ascend a steep hill. Like scenes from a dream, the open wildness of the stretch changes abruptly to the insular mysteriousness of a forest. The road winds its way through a stand of small trees, curiously all the same height, perhaps a result of the force of the wind from the ocean below.

The road curves unexpectedly, perfect for letting go in a fast car. The trees so close, the speed feels more intense. Exhilarating—darkness, speed, the unknown looming around every blind curve. I feel myself pulled by a force I can't name.

Descending now. Suddenly, like the revelatory part of a dream, the ocean appears before me—so vast, engulfing, that the scattered motels and houses along its edge seem like cut-out pictures, pasted on.

Not a soul to be seen, all the summer sojourners long gone. I glance at the dashboard clock: 11 p.m. Approaching the Memory Motel, a red neon light in the dark window announcing BAR is the only light on. I suddenly feel great fatigue, coming down from the frenzy of my ride. I wonder if it's open; it's the kind of place that looks neither open nor closed. And are the memories you experience there from your past or new ones you take home with you?

My mind flashes back to a story I read in a local paper a few years ago, about a college student who had hung herself from the rafters of a Montauk motel, in late September when all the other summer people had gone back to their real places and lives. Maybe it had been here, at the Memory Motel, the waves of painful memories in the end drowning out her dreams of the future.

Panic begins to shoot through my veins. I press down hard on the pedal, blurring past a stretch of motels, restaurants and gas stations, entering an expanse of sky and trees again.

Almost at the end now, I can feel it. The sky's opening up, the ocean's pounding sound is filling my head, my heart, rushing through my veins. I see a dirt path to the side, pull over and turn off the car which heaves an almost audible sigh at ending its hard journey. As I step out into the air, the wind slams the car door against me, almost pushing me back into my seat. How thrilling to feel the power of wind!

Walking with head bowed along the path toward a cliff in the near distance, I feel the wind's force increasing. Wouldn't it be a great way to go if suddenly the atoms in my body broke into little fragments merging with the wind?

As I approach the cliff, the ocean's pounding sound below drowns out the sound of the wind. Standing at the edge now, I close my eyes and hear the sea making a circle, beginning as a faraway deep hidden rumbling, building in a crescendo until it reaches a climax, crashing in upon itself, then receding out to the dark depths to begin its journey all over again. I feel strangely comforted by this sound: that in this constant circling, life has no end.

I open my eyes. The moonlight shining upon the sea's surface creates a bright pathway amidst the darkness, as if inviting me to follow. Below me the waves crash spiritedly upon the huge rocks, sending spumes of water up the face of the steep cliff. I look around me: no trees, no bushes, only a scattering of beach grass clinging to the edge.

I lean back my head and close my eyes.

Like a piece of flotsam from the wreck of my life, a vague image of Katherine floats before me. I quickly push it away. I picture my office desk and well-worn leather chair, but they quickly drift from view, too. Snapshots of my parents come into focus: father with his stern brow and strongly set jaw, although not wearing his black gown, looking as always like the all-powerful judge; mother, her slightly cloudy blue eyes and sweet but sad smile, masking some well-kept secret inside. Now they drift away with the other images.

No other face flashes before me except, curiously, that of a black Labrador I had from the time I was three to the age of seventeen. How I loved that creature, my closest companion, the explorations we went on in the woods near our home, the fishing in the bay in the spring and hunting in the fall.

Suddenly a great sadness comes over me. A deep longing wells up, from some forgotten place, for the land of my youth, for the beauty, solace and adventure I found there. Standing on this cliff, I'm transposed in time, walking with my dog in the woods. How strange it's still there, almost intact: that humbling yet thrilling mystery and power of the woods and call to explore; that fully alive feeling on the edge of knowing and not knowing—heart pounding, eyes seeing everything everywhere, body both tense and relaxed, ready to receive as well as respond; and the intimation of an infinite otherness out there, yet simultaneously of it being in me, of animal, man and woods as one.

Looking down at the water now, I imagine a bridge linking this piece of land and time to that piece of my youth, and the water underneath the bridge all the time, faces and events between that moment long ago and this one right now, churning together, culminating in one crash upon the black rocks.

I close my eyes again as I listen to the wind and the waves. I hear their voices: the deep bass and underlying rhythm of the waves, and above it, the alto and riffing melody of the wind. They're outside of me, but now I hear them inside. I try to decipher the lyrics of this song, yet hear no words. A kind of spiraling joy and plummeting sadness come over me all at once.

A picture takes shape in my mind: I see myself as a boy, bright and shining like a star, inside of a dark body that's me as a grown man; and then I see that small bright boy grow larger, until he fills out to the dark periphery of the man, turning it into a yellow shimmering line.

I open my eyes. The moon is fading in the western sky and the sun is rising up out of the ocean.

Running Aground

Journal entry, October 30:
   I'm writing on the first page of a journal I bought before I left the city last night. Maybe I can write myself into a whole new story.

   Who shall I be? What shall I do? Is it really possible to create a new life for myself, as a novelist creates a character in a book? That there is no old story to go back to—Katherine, the law firm, the apartment—is clear.

   Could I just be no one for a while, choose no particular life until what life I want is revealed? Be kind of an invisible man? This just may be the perfect place to be invisible, too: Montauk—The End, The Last Resort, as the bumper stickers so apocalyptically proclaim. You might think that a city with its multitudes of people milling about would be the ideal setting for anonymity. And, in contrast, a place like this of so few people, one wandering soul would stick out that much more. But here, man fades into the stronger background of nature, which seems the right place for me to be now.

   What about what I should do? One can't just be. Strange, I don't remember ever wondering what I might do with the hours in a day: up and to work until 6:30, dinner with Katherine, usually some more work before bed; on weekends, tennis Saturday morning at the club, an opera, play, concert or museum outing planned by Katherine. And that was it.

The only time I thought about what I might do with my time was our two week-vacation in the winter and summer. But usually I let Katherine plan that, too. Whatever she wanted was fine with me. Work and Katherine: that's what all the hours in all my days ...

A dizzying sense of slipping off a ledge with nothing there to brake the fall, a sickening feeling of something inside like an invisible cord being cut from its life-source outside, come over me. How can I begin to replace all that was there, an entire accumulated life—all the work, the people, the things, the time? Everything behind me, nothing ahead, nothing ...

My hand's shaking so hard, I put down the pen and journal on the bed and close my eyes. If I sleep some, maybe I'll feel better. I haven't slept for a very long time.

Lulled by the ocean's lapping waves a few stone throws away, I drift off.

I'm on a raft, a gusty wind blowing me closer and closer to a brown and green land I see off in the distance. I fight with the sail, try to change the raft's course. But the wind is the stronger. Surrendering, I let myself be taken. I wonder what will I find there—people, animals, anything? The raft runs aground on some black rocks on the shore and, just as I climb off, a wave smashes it to pieces. Standing on the shoreline, I watch the pieces wash up alongside me. They are too broken. I can't possibly make them whole again. I turn to the green forest, then to the sea and start walking toward it. Suddenly I hear a voice, calling from the forest. I turn around.

I awake with a start.

"Excuse me, sir. I didn't think anyone was here. I always come to clean the rooms at noon."

The room is dark, all the blinds being closed. Light emanates from the doorway where the person's backlit figure appears silhouetted, shining out to me from what feels like a galaxy away.

"I'll come back later."

The door closes. I imagine I'm still dreaming. I move my hands slowly over the contours of my face.

I get out of bed and look at my watch on the bureau. Only 15 hours since I left the city. Incredible! It feels more like 15 days.

Okay. Get a grip. The journal. I should finish what I started.

What to do: what have I wanted to do and never gotten around to? I've thought for a long time about re-reading all the philosophy books I read in college, curious to see years later what they might mean to me.

Good. What else? Play the trumpet. I've often thought about buying a trumpet and playing again, as I did when I was a boy and in college. Okay. Those won't take up all the hours in a day. Of course lots of walks—along the ocean every day, in the woods. Do some fishing, which I once loved to do. Maybe even learn how to surf, something I always intended doing on our summer trips to the Hamptons but never got around to. Of course it's not exactly the right time of year, but I'll just get a wet suit, be really daring. Maybe I could get a dog. Find a nice cottage on the beach. Fine. What else?

My mind goes blank. I stare at my hand poised with pen upon paper. That's it!

I've always wanted to write stories. It's been so long buried, I couldn't easily recall it. Way back, before college, I loved writing stories, especially after being in the woods with my dog—adventure stories. I remember my mother thought one was so good she wanted to send it off to *Reader's Digest*. But I wouldn't let her. And then … college, law school, marriage, no time.

Maybe I can't even do it: all these years of legal writing, enough to cramp a Faulkner or Melville. But maybe not, if I reach way down, way back—and way forward?

What should I write about? Enough, enough questions and answers for now! A rap at the door again. I open it.

"I'm sorry to bother you, sir. If you're going to stay another day, I'll tell the manager. But if you are leaving today, he said I must tell you that it's past the check-out time."

"Yes, of course. I lost track of the time. Um, I suppose I will stay another day, maybe more. I'm going to be looking for a place to live, so I'll need to stay here in the meantime."

"Fine, I'll tell him." Her voice is a kind of exaggerated whisper, her eyes are a burnt sienna nearly matching her skin, and her dark hair is pulled back from her startlingly beautiful face.

"Yes, thank you. Can you tell me where I might find a store to buy toothpaste, that sort of thing, and a place to get something to eat?"

"As you go out the front door, on the corner is a drug store, and next to that is a restaurant, one of the few opened at this time of year."

"Thanks."

Emerging from the motel, I find a glorious autumn day, the kind in which the air is so crisp and the light so pure that all seems sculpted, as if in a hyper-reality.

I decide to go for a walk first, cross the street from the motel and walk out to the ocean dunes. Blades of beach grass blowing in the wind trace spiraling patterns in the sand. I marvel at the delicate designs and their ephemeral nature. With rain or a stronger wind, these lines in the sand will disappear. But then they'll reappear, at least as long as the beach grass is still here. It's probably already been here for thousands of years, as the dunes in which it lives have, too. How brief and inconsequential my little life seems, like this temporary tracing upon the sand.

Yet, maybe by listening to a different wind blowing through my life, I'll bend, like this blade of grass, in a new direction, and from that center create new traces.

Walking out onto the white sanded beach, I look to the east. After a short stretch of motels and condos, for the next several miles only a few scattered houses appear perched on the bluffs, then the land disappears around a curve to the north, at the end of which is Montauk Point. That's where I want to live, somewhere along that stretch.

The tide looks to be at its lowest ebb, so the beach is wide enough to walk as far as I can see. Two gulls squawk above me, apparently arguing over a delectable morsel dangling from one bird's beak. A ways out over the water, a small flock of cormorants, a bird that made an impression upon me in my youth for its strange, prehistoric appearance, is heading due east. Startling rust-orange colored cliffs, deeply gashed by wind and water, rise nearly straight up about 80 feet on one side of me and on the other, spray from the ocean's surge upon the shore's rocks creates a misty veil through which I move. In places, the beach between the water and cliffs narrows to only a couple of feet, giving my journey a certain thrilling edge of danger. Even if it is only the danger of getting wet fully clothed at the end of October, I nevertheless feel that quickening-pulse-excitement of doing something a little dangerous. What do I ever do that's even this marginally risky?

A wave crashes hard against a massive rock nearby. I recall the dream of the raft breaking upon the rocks, of my choosing to turn back to the sea until I heard a voice.

As I face toward the spray and close my eyes, the water rains down upon me. Licking the salty drops from my lips, I realize that coming here, leaving everything behind, is the riskiest thing I've ever done.

Heading east, I see off in the near distance, perched on a bluff, exactly where I want to live. Stairs lead down to the beach. I walk toward them and, looking up, see that the house is made of stone. It sits almost precariously near the edge, a Tudor-style dwelling that seems quite small, compared to the mansions I've past along the ocean. I climb the nearly vertical stairs to the top.

No one appears to be around, but I hesitate to walk onto the little patch of grass surrounding the house. The stones, with their orange-brown tone, look as if they might have come from here. Two large chimneys, lots of windows, and no other houses nearby: the perfect place.

I make a wish.

Sounds of Silence

The ocean is calm today. Gazing out the window, I feel a calm seeping into me, a sense of my outer and inner worlds coming into sync.

On one table alongside me are the philosophy books I bought at a local bookstore, my journal, spiral-bound notebooks for other writing, and on another, the trumpet I found in a second-hand shop in a nearby town. The house is furnished with some of the most interesting furniture I've ever seen. The owner of the house, away for the winter, is a musician who also makes Shaker-style furniture with an individual flair. The starkly simple yet elegant Shaker lines are there, but the wood is embellished with curved and linear designs, reminding me of the natural surroundings: the linearity of the deeply carved bluffs below and the undulating lines of the ocean beyond. The stone house itself feels like an organic outgrowth of its environment and has a romantic, poetic quality, which I hope will inspire me. Indeed, I was told by the realtor that it was designed by the famous architect Grosvenor Atterbury in 1912 for the poet Rosina Hoyt Hoppin, and, over the years, had been rented to such romantic figures as Marilyn Monroe.

Nobody knows where I am. The telephone sits silently. If I were at my desk at work, I would have talked on the phone with ten different people by this time of day, noon. Talking, talking, all day long, with clients, other lawyers, in court: an endless torrent of words. And then there's the unceasing noise of the city: even enclosed in a skyscraper on the 25th floor, I was never completely free of the sounds. How strange and wonderful this silence is!

As if the blind on a window is suddenly drawn, a new sense of space and light opens up in this silence. Images, words appear like clouds drifting by, luring me to make them into some kind of form. I eagerly reach for a notebook, but staring at the blank page, I suddenly freeze up. What is the premise? Then what follows that? The linear thinking, methodical mind automatically kicks in and tries to pre-empt this inchoate voice from finding form. I close my eyes and hear the crashing of the waves beyond, curling in and around, give myself over to this sound. In the upward surge, I imagine I hear the word "life" and in the descending surge and crash, the word "death." I open my eyes and write quickly:

In the silence between the waves,
between the rising and the falling, the deep dark rumblings
and shining moments,
listen to the sound of life unbound.
Is it here you'll find that for which you're yearning?
Still, still that clamorous churning!

I read it. Did I really write this? It's hard to believe. It sounds so—not like me, so naïve and kind of fuzzily mystical. Stop being so critical! Before I can feel free enough to write anything with emotional life and depth to it I first have to quiet that self-censoring voice.

The telephone rings, startling me. Who could be calling? Oh yes, there's one person who knows where I am, the beautiful woman Mariah who worked at the motel.

"Hello. Yes, Mariah. Tomorrow will be fine."

She'll be coming to clean my house tomorrow. With the motels closing for the winter, she needs to find other work. She's trying to save money, between cleaning houses and waitressing at night, to finish her college education. I sense something special about her and want to help her.

It suddenly occurs to me I should call my office, let someone know my extended weekend has now been extended indefinitely. Nobody knew anything desperate was going on with me; I think I effectively hid it from everyone, except perhaps from Madeline, my secretary, who always seemed to know when something was wrong with me. Strange how, even though we rarely shared any words of a personal nature, there was an unspoken trust and bond between us. I won't have to explain a lot to her: I'm on sabbatical for my mental health. My partners can handle my caseload or, if they wish, hire someone to take my place. I'm sorry for any inconvenience this may cause them or my clients, but there's nothing else I can do.

Picking up my trumpet, I glide my hand over its golden, gleaming curves. Gingerly, my fingers press down on the valves: such a beautifully spare instrument, its design so compact, these three brass valves capable of a full spectrum of sound. I think of the poem I just wrote and imagine how the words would translate into sounds. Placing my lips to the mouthpiece, I concentrate and try to hear the sounds between the crashing waves.

Runs with the Wind

I'm reading Heidegger's *Being and Time* and wondering how I understood this tome, or thought I did, when I read it at 20 years old. Perhaps I don't possess the keen powers of comprehension for this complexity of thought as I did then? Or is it that, after 20 years, these theories that once sounded so elegant, persuasive and of greatest importance to understanding the "big questions about life" now seem to be quite inexplicably irrelevant to life as it actually is? Maybe the problem is not so much with the ideas themselves as it is with the dense and ponderous manner in which they're expressed, as if to purposely obfuscate: "If to interpret the meaning of Being becomes our task, Dasein [Being-there] is not only the primary entity to be interrogated; it is also that entity which already comports itself, in its Being, towards what we are asking about when we ask this question."

The other possible explanation for not understanding these words and ideas at the moment is that I can't give them the concentration they require, distracted as I am by the presence of Mariah in the other room. However, it's not a distraction caused by any noise she's creating, but rather the lack of it, her manner of moving as quiet and subtle as her manner of speaking, as if she's floating just above the hard surface of things.

"Excuse me, Mr. Collins. Is there anything else you'd like me to do before I leave?" Not hearing her approach from the other room, her voice startles me.

"No, I don't think so."

"When shall I come again?"

"How about next week, same time? Come, sit down for a moment while I write you a check."

She walks to the bay window where I'm sitting and looks out at the ocean. "Have you found that the sound of the ocean has changed the way you think yet?" She says this without turning around, as if she knows it's true and is simply asking me to verify. "I found that even when I'm away from it, I can hear its echo, creating a kind of rhythmic background in my life. When events in your life become overwhelming, it's good to have this sense that things come and they go."

She turns now from the window and looks straight into my eyes with her soft but so penetrating eyes. Is she challenging me to respond? Unaccustomed to having such open conversations, particularly with someone I've just met, I'm unnerved.

"Actually," she says, eyes now looking off to the side of me, "I hear two different echoes of water, one of the ocean and one of a lively stream. The latter is always the louder, for my people, the Montauks, lived closer to a stream than the ocean. But now that sound is silent."

"Why is that?"

"Our land was taken from us long ago. Then houses were built, driveways paved and wells dug, so our streams dried up. Coming from artesian springs, the water was once so pure that, according to historical accounts, the settlers coveted it for what they believed were its great healing properties." She's silent for a moment. "Maybe when we get our land back, we'll be able to bring back the streams."

"You're getting your land back?"

"We're attempting to. But first we have to establish ourselves as a recognized tribe. That's the reason I've come back here and one of the reasons I've gone back to college—to get a law degree."

"I see. Good for you. What had you studied before?"

"Fine arts, with a specialty in photography. It's difficult to make a living as a fine art photographer, so I had been working for an ad agency in Manhattan. But I grew disenchanted with that life after too many years and decided to come back here, to get away and think about what I might do next. Then, after talking to my relatives, it became clear. I still do some free-lance work, but in order to live part of the time here and help pay for college, I do work like this, because, besides waitressing, there's not much else out here. I don't mind though, because for once in my life I feel I really know what I want to do."

"How do you find studying law after fine arts?"

"At first, law seemed confining compared to art. But I'm beginning to see how one approach can help the other, how the more emotional and philosophical sensibilities of the artist can be very helpful to the reason-and-fact-oriented sensibility of the lawyer, and vice versa."

I nod my head, looking into her eyes, but then quickly turn away. "Yes, I think I know what you mean, Mariah. I'm a lawyer who's trying to develop some of that other sensibility which, I suppose, is one valid explanation for why I'm here."

"I thought you might be a lawyer."

"How could you tell?"

"Well, lawyers just seem to have a certain way of speaking—very precise, controlled, with lots of terms like 'valid explanation,'" she smiles playfully, not sarcastically, "and with a self-assuredness that sometimes masks a kind of fear—of what they don't know and of their emotions that, like an ocean, pound at their bluffs of reason. I've learned this from listening to some of my friends who are lawyers."

Never have I met anyone this direct before, yet it's a directness that's not offensive but rather intriguing, stimulating.

"By the way, you can call me by my real name, Oshanta."

"Oshanta. What a lovely-sounding name, a little like… the sound of the wind."

Her eyes widen. "In the language of the Montauk, Oshanta means Runs with the Wind."

We stare at each other momentarily, as if we had bumped into each other in the dark. I quickly avert my eyes, fixing my attention on the ocean beyond.

Voices of the Earth

Journal entry, November 8:
I knew Katherine would return to haunt me, that my not thinking about her much since coming out here was more the effect of my highly developed ability to block out bad things. Today I've decided I can't fight it anymore—how did Oshanta put it?—emotions like an ocean that forever pound at the bluffs of reason.

But how could I have not seen the end coming? When I picture us sitting at the dinner table talking about our respective days at our respective law offices, musing upon a certain person or discussing a particular legal point, sipping our wine and perhaps briefly reflecting upon how harmonious a life this was, it seems as if our lives had taken on an illusory quality, as if we were acting in a little play, pretending to be the real Katherine and Paul, and didn't know that we were, or at least I didn't. And the further along we continued in this play, the harder it was to see or want to see what we were doing, the play having taken on a dramatic momentum of its own. Then, without any warning, the end came. Why didn't she ever tell me something was wrong? How could it be that people can spend years pretending to be happy? Maybe if we'd ...

I see an image of a child, a girl, with Katherine's blue eyes and my reddish-brown hair, her fair skin and delicate nose, my long limbs. She laughs easily, suddenly, like Katherine, twirls the end of her hair when she's thinking hard, her head tilted to the right, hair flowing over her shoulder; when she's happy, she'll twitch her foot excitedly, and when she's sad ...

Overwhelmed by things that were not what they seemed and things that should have been but never were, I put down my pen. I pick up my trumpet and, just as I start to play, there's a knock at my door. Who could it be? It's not Oshanta's day to come, but it could only be her. I open the door.

"Hello, Paul. I hope I'm not disturbing you."

"No, not at all, Oshanta."

"You mentioned that you enjoy going for walks and that you'd like to see the land where the Montauks once lived. I'm going for a walk there now—it's only a short ways from here—and thought I'd ask you to join me."

"Yes, well, all right, Oshanta. It might be good for me to get out."

We travel down the driveway to the road, cross it and enter a state park. There're a number of buildings, one large old farmhouse and a barn beginning to cave in in the middle. The surrounding landscape is open and mostly horizontal, its rolling greenish brown hills only occasionally sprouting a small clump of windswept sycamores and strange, small trees I don't know the name of. We walk closer to one and stand underneath it. Though it's delicate and graceful in form, buried within its tangled web of branches that appears like a wild and frenzied crown are two-inch long dangerous looking thorns.

"A strange kind of beauty, isn't it?" Oshanta says. "It's a hawthorn tree and one of the few native varieties. The Montauketts used these thorns to make sewing needles." She reaches up and breaks one off, handing it to me.

"It makes me think of the Crown of Thorns." Not realizing how sharp the thorn is, I prick my finger, drawing a drop of blood.

"Yes. That's a powerful image, and maybe explains why Native Americans, who were forbidden by the white settlers from worshiping their own gods, often didn't have a lot of trouble accepting the symbol and meaning of the crucifixion of Christ. Of course, I think the irony was lost on white men."

"Irony?"

"The irony of Native Americans, who suffered so at the hands of white men, accepting the central spiritual symbol of the settlers: a tortured and suffering man whose primary message was to do unto others as you would have them do unto you."

"Yes, I understand what you're saying." I look up again at the top of the tree. "I was fairly religious as a boy, and even thought seriously of becoming a priest. But I couldn't reconcile the terrible things Christians did in the name of their religion with what the religion preached."

She follows my gaze upward to the tree's crown. "It's interesting how our different historical references, the needle and the Crown of Thorns, reveal our opposite ways of seeing the world: the Native Americans' spiritual and moral beliefs come from the material earth itself, so there's no disparity between the world of spirit and the world of matter; while western civilization's comes from the mind of man, the stuff of his dreams and ideals. It's also a difference between being thankful for what is, and longing always for what isn't."

She turns to me and looks straight into my eyes with that gently penetrating, inquisitive gaze.

"Yes, I think you're right. Perhaps this explains our terrible destructiveness, too: that we are detached from our feelings toward the earth, and maybe, by extension, toward ourselves." It seems suddenly as if some kind of tightness inside me—around my lungs, my heart?—loosens its grip and I can breathe more deeply.

We begin to walk up a hill. "This is the land of my ancestors, the land of the Montauketts." She sweeps her arm in a panorama. "In the 1600s in the time of our great sachem, Wyandanch, the Montauketts were the leaders among the 13 native communities on Long Island, or Paumanok in our language, which means fish for the shape of the Island. It was once very wooded, then the settlers came and grazed their sheep and cattle on it, every year taking more of it for themselves until the Montauketts became useful tenants—of our own land—as tenders of the settlers' herds."

We leave behind the open rolling fields and enter a path through an area dense with small trees and bushes which Oshanta names for me: high-bush blueberry, wild grape, sumac, cat briar. Soon the low-growing brush gives way to a more vertical landscape, to groves of trees, their leaves having reached their peak of autumn reds and yellows and now beginning to turn brown and fall to the ground.

The path begins to wind its way subtly around the side of a hill, the sense of ascending only noticeable if I turn around to see from where we'd come. The tall trunks of white oaks rise to the sky around us. Oshanta touches the bark of one.

"I find it's good to touch a tree or something growing in the earth once in a while. It gives us a sense of belonging we sometimes so desperately need."

I touch it, too, feel its hard grooves, my eyes following the white-gray bark upward to the crown of leaves gently rustling in the wind. I wonder at its strength, what it has endured through the seasons, through its span of time on earth.

We continue on the narrow path bordered by shimmering emerald green patches of moss. Arising languidly out of the wetlands below are lovely trees—swamp maples, Oshanta tells me—their full graceful branches giving them a kind of feminine appearance, perfect counterparts to the sturdy, masculine oaks. Their branches move together touching now and then in the rhythm of the wind.

Scattered incongruously amidst the trees are occasional huge gray-white rocks, remains of a glacial age. Delicate lichen of a subtle green hue caresses the rock, softening its hard exterior. Oshanta places her palm upon one.

"My ancestors believed that a spiritual force, Manito, dwelled in all things, from rocks to trees, birds to people. And if you listen closely enough, you can hear the spirits' voices. But it demands a different kind of listening than we're used to, one that requires much forgetting and, at the same time, remembering about ourselves."

Placing my hand on the rock, I try to imagine how it arrived on this plot of ground, imagine mountain-sized boulders moving across the land, everything blindingly bright from the snow and ice.

"I cannot yet always hear the spirits speak. I'm still learning," Oshanta says softly. "My great aunt taught me a poem, told to her by her father, of the spirit of a giant rock, like this one, speaking. Would you like to hear it?"

"Yes."

The Last Resort

I am hard and my surface is cold.
Some say there is only this,
but in truth, powerful spirit and long memory live inside.
As I am ages older than the Oak and once singing Stream,
within these hard edges many stories I hold
of the great creatures who in these woods dwelled
and now are no more.
The Eagle who once soared overhead like a watchful
winged god;
The Wolf whose voice, so searching and sad,
still haunts the night air; and the Men who once passed
this way,
looks of wide wonder in their eyes,
who touched me and heard what I had to say.

Then came the Men who could not see or hear above the
sound of the machines
they carried through these woods to clear.
But I could hear the cries of the tall Oaks as they fell, tears
of the once lively Streams as they lost their sweet songs,
cries of the dying Bald Eagle, Gray Fox and Heath Hen—
Oh, how these cries all sound like those of a small child, as
if we had come from the same Mother, way back when!

But it is the saddest for me, for I alone have been through
it all,
this deep break in my ancient wall
not made from the forces of Nature over thousands of years
but from the cries of my Friends.
I cannot know how it will all end, but I always have hope
for, every now and then, someone will touch me and hear
me among Men.

Voices of the Ancestors

Continuing along the path, we come to a wooden bridge that crosses over a stream.

"See how this stream is barely moving? Thirty years ago, when I walked here as a little girl, it was very lively. The pollution from too many homes along the edge of Lake Montauk to the west, which feeds into this stream, and from too many boats in the Lake have nearly put an end to it."

The path ascends and soon we come out onto a circular plateau covered with high honey-colored wild grass. Off to the northern end lie rock formations, what look to be remains of a structure. A large hawthorn tree, almost completely imprisoned by wild vines, stands in the center of the plateau. Protected by the surrounding woods, it's almost an eerily still and quiet place.

"This is where my ancestors dwelled. Over there you can see Big Reed Pond, and to the northeast beyond the woods lies Oyster Pond, and beyond that, Block Island Sound. They had everything they needed here to live: fish, fowl, deer, berries, water and wood, and they grew corn, squash and beans over there. These rock formations are the only remains of the village; the last homes were burned down in the late 1800s by a developer named Arthur Benson in his attempt to drive the last handful of Montauks off the small patch of land they had been reduced to, here in Indian Fields. Even one of our sachems, King David Hannibal Pharaoh, and his wife burned to death in their home here in 1839. The last of my people were forced to leave, joining the others who had already left beginning a century before, to parts of East Hampton, upstate New York, and even as far as Wisconsin.

> *A sound is heard throughout our land,*
> *a moaning, yearning cry;*
> *"Oh mighty Arm of Right stretch forth, Crush out our*
> *hopeless misery.*
> *I see a weary dark-skinned race*
> *Bend low beneath Oppression's weight ..."*
> *I hear an agonizing cry*
> *Hushed by the cruel fiery flame.*
> *I see the home left desolate,*
> *I see a father forced to die, I hear a mother's anguished*
> *groan, I hear their children's piteous cry.*
> *How long I ask shall these things be?*
> *How long shall men have hearts of stone? ...*
> *Great God ... Declare this evil shall not be ...*

"That is from a poem, 'The Nation's Evil,' written by a Montaukett writer named Olivia Ward Bush Banks in the early part of the twentieth century. I always think of it when I come here."

The wind, like a voice from far away, rustles through the surrounding trees. I imagine I hear the cries of those who once dwelled here as they watched in terror and grief their homes and earthly belongings burn in the treacherous flames, the cries of King David Hannibal Pharaoh and his wife. Their voices come closer, now echoing off the wall of stones like a chorus in a Greek tragedy bearing witness to past transgressions and whispering of a future when they might be avenged. Oshanta is listening to the wind, too.

"Of all the elements here, wind is the most constant. At the end of a peninsula as it is, Montauk is never without some wind—from the ocean, from the Block Island Sound. Our prayers were always directed to the four cardinal points, which we called the four winds. Our most sacred winds are from the east, for light and life, and the west, for rain and where our spirits go when we die. We had other sacred spirits: of the sea, sun, earth, fire, and corn. But our prayers were not complete if we didn't pray to the four winds. This was traditionally done with tobacco, a sacred plant to Native Americans, though a handful of earth can be used in its place."

Oshanta bends forward and carefully uproots a handful of grass. "It's been a while since I've been here, and I should pay my respects. You see, I was given the special name, Runs with the Wind, for a reason. According to my great aunt, who is about 90 years old and lives not far from here, the name was chosen for me because I would someday help to bring our tribe, now scattered in the four directions, together again onto this land, its ancestral land. I've been entrusted with an important task by my ancestors. If you'd like, you can join me."

I hesitate, my Episcopal upbringing causing me to regard this ritual rather skeptically. But then I feel not joining her would be comparable to not participating in church when the priest says, "Let us pray." I join her in taking a handful of grass.

We stand first to the east. Oshanta holds her hand high and closes her eyes. "Thank you, Manito of the East, for shining your light down upon the earth helping all things to grow and us to see the way we need to go." She draws her hand to her heart, then raises it again and drops a sprinkle of grass. I do the same.

She turns to the south, giving thanks for soft winds and warmth, to the west for rain, and to the north for snow and cold to strengthen our spirits to overcome adversity. A red-tailed hawk that had followed us overhead along the path now appears circling above the hawthorn tree, making a high-pitched "kee-kee" sound. We watch his graceful gliding.

"A beautiful bird. Once many hawks flew here and eagles, too, a sacred bird to Native American tribes. In our cosmology, the Thunderer is the guardian of the heavens, and the Thunderbird, another name for eagle and our most sacred symbol, is his helper who provides the healing rain; lightning is the flashing of his eye and thunder the noise of his wings."

It seems a perfect ending to the ceremony: a majestic bird, much like the Montauks' sacred bird, joining the four directions into the form of a circle.

Suddenly the wind picks up and the rustling through the trees becomes noticeably louder.

"This may sound strange, but I feel the spirits of my ancestors are here," Oshanta says in a hushed voice.

Watching the branches of the trees moving in the wind, I try to imagine the presence of something unseen.

Oshanta, facing toward the west and the setting sun, closes her eyes. "I'm envisioning them now, right above the tops of the trees. There are three of them: an older man, a woman and a younger man."

> *We come to you, Runs with the Wind, from the far-away place in the sky*
> *where our souls have found peace and rest.*
> *We come here where the earth and the sky, the world of what is and what could be meet.*

Oshanta says these words methodically, as if she were merely the mouthpiece for another's voice.

> *I am Wyandanch, first sachem of the once great Montauk who ruled over this land we loved like our mother, this beautiful, bountiful fish-shaped Paumanok.*
> *We offered our hands and a share of our land to the men who came like pale gods from the sea.*
> *But not good men were they who stole from us and told us lies.*
> *We did not know why this was so, for vast was this rich earth, the useful plants, the creatures of land and sea.*
> *We were even forced to beg wood for our fires, while they cut clear to the sea to graze cows and sheep.*
> *And many of us died terrible deaths, fevers and poxes stealing our last breaths.*
> *Our spirits broken, we scattered far and wide, only a few of us remaining nearby.*
> *Now it is time for the wounded body of the Montauk to heal.*

> *I am Queen Maria, your great great aunt, and I want you to know it is time again for a woman to lead,*
> *to carry forth the fight for our land,*
> *stolen from us through devious deeds.*

*We confronted the white man, but were wrongly denied,
as Judge Blackmar looked us in the eye on that day in his
court in 1909, and told us as a people we did not exist.
With our money spent fighting in court, and me growing
weary and old, we were left to wait for another day, and
that day is now here.*

*I am your great great uncle, Stephen Pharaoh.
It is not out of hate we make claim against white men, but
out of love of the land and the creatures being hurt
by men who want to rule over every last foot of earth,
as if it is Nature—or is it themselves?—they hate.
So many miles of earth did I walk, through dark, quiet
woods and sunlit fields, so like my friends they became,
that I know with the power of words
they would say 'Walk more lightly upon me, I pray.'
We know the world must change,
but we know by honoring the earth's living things
a better world we can make.*

After a few moments of silence, Oshanta opens her eyes. They look as if she's not sure where she is, or perhaps what she's just experienced. Then her eyes begin to clear.

The sun is falling behind the trees. Without speaking, we begin to walk back along the trail.

The Will to Power

The experience with Oshanta in the woods, one of the most profound and mysterious of my life, keeps coming back to me. How did she come to speak those words? The image of Judge Blackmar looking the Montauks in their eyes and proclaiming as a people they did not exist, is, as a lawyer, particularly vivid to me. I can just picture this judge, whose name seems so fitting it sounds fictitious, sitting in judgment at his altar, like a God clad in black—why do judges wear black, anyway? why not white or perhaps a neutral gray?—telling the room full of Montauks, their eyes wide but sad with a look of hope crossed with sudden disappointment and disbelief, that he saw no Montauks in the room, denying the reality before him.

Then *"...men who want to rule over every last foot of earth, as if it is Nature—or is it themselves?—they hate,"* are the other words that most resonate in my mind, though I must give them more thought as I don't fully grasp their meaning.

As part of my philosophical re-education, I'm re-reading Nietzsche's *The Will to Power*. More than any other philosopher, his ideas held a fascination for me in my college days, some ideas about which I now see a certain perversity: his disdain for compassion and sympathy, which he saw as "insipid" emotions; and his belief in a system divided between those few "noble" men of will and courage who are meant to lead and dominate over that vast majority of weak, unimaginative followers. Why did he appeal so strongly to me and my philosophy major colleagues? Perhaps it was that, at that age, we were struggling for some sense of power and control, over ourselves and the emerging world we were one step into. And a key aspect of Nietzsche's philosophy, with its impassioned call to seize one's latent strengths and transform them into conscious action in the world, offered a clear and romantically appealing route to gaining confidence at that difficult stage.

None of my friends was so taken with Nietzsche as Jonathan. Jonathan was brilliant, terribly shy and self-conscious. He was rather small and had wiry, cork-screw blondish hair that refused to lie flat on his head, as if the electricity of his brain's synapses made it that way. His gray-blue eyes looked always wild and lost. When Jonathan discovered Nietzsche, it was as if he found the Holy Grail. Transformed overnight, he became suddenly extroverted, self-confident, to the point of aggressiveness, and absolutely evangelistic in spreading the good word about Nietzsche: He had the secret answer to our adolescent fears and weaknesses, and you can actually will yourself into believing you are chosen for greatness. But, of course, only a few would be called to this greatness, and Jonathan was selective about whom he preached to.

One drizzly, stormy, unusually cold April—I remember it was right around Easter—he invited me to a party, very exclusive, he said, by which I knew he meant intellectually so, for Jonathan was far from the socially elite at Yale. He was on a full scholarship and he never talked about his parents.

The party was on the lower west side of Manhattan, in the neighborhood where he lived. I walked in to this dark, cave-like apartment, lit only by candles. On the brick walls hung a plain rectangular mirror and an ornate gold-framed photograph of Nietzsche, the famous one taken later in his life in which there's a touch of madness in his eyes. There were only two other people besides Jonathan: a woman, dressed all in black with dyed red hair and a face that was made up like an actor in Noh theatre, powdery white with lots of black around the eyes and bright red lips; and a tall thin man who was also dressed in black and whose face looked like a Noh mask, too.

Jonathan's eyes were the wildest I'd ever seen them. He had a spaced-out frozen grin which was a strange mix of terror and glee. He offered me some LSD: it would help me to see the real God, Zarathustra, who would talk to me as he was talking to Jonathan right then, telling him that if he wanted to he could conquer the world. Shadows cast by the candlelight of Jonathan and his two guests loomed on the cold brick walls. Nietzsche's face glowered with its own sepulchral light. A sickening smell of musty incense burned. Although my immediate impulse was to bolt out of there, something in this dark, nauseating power was holding me. I stared at the LSD in his hand.

"Don't be afraid. Don't you want to be enlightened, all of your fears and illusions stripped away?" I looked far into his eyes. He was willing his power over me, his eyes pulling me in, his face, like Nietzsche's, a nexus of life and death. I tore myself away and ran out the door.

A week later back in school, I didn't see Jonathan around. He never came back, and no one seemed to know what had happened to him.

Avoiding reflecting on this subject all these years, I think I felt somehow responsible for Jonathan's fate, whatever it may have been. Maybe if I'd been less afraid, I would have interpreted the situation correctly. I would have grasped that, rather than feeling powerful and invincible, Jonathan was in a state of sheer terror. I could have brought him back from the edge, taken the LSD from his palm and held his hand for a moment and said—I'm not sure, maybe nothing. Maybe just a look of understanding and compassion instead of fear in my face would have been enough.

I see now that in someone like Jonathan, this combination of a powerful hallucinogenic drug and an obsession with the more extreme aspects of Nietzsche's philosophy was very dangerous, perhaps even putting him over the edge. He used the drug to help convince himself he was a true Nietzschean superman. But one can't develop an inner sense of power by simply latching on to a theory—and one certainly can't do it with the aid of drugs. A philosophy for living has to be *lived* to become real. Also, what I didn't grasp then is that this Nietzschean power and courage are built on one of the most potentially destructive, and most common, forms of fear: that one must conquer what one doesn't understand.

The words of Oshanta's ancestors become clearer now. Just as Jonathan didn't develop the inner mechanism to control his own power—willing it instead—we as a society have not evolved the moral mechanism to understand and take responsibility for the power of our creations, willing them upon the world—*"as if it is Nature—or is it themselves?—they hate."* The more we impose our will to a detrimental effect upon our surroundings, the more separated we become from our inner-self, a self that probably has some sense of balance within nature. And the more separated we become, the more we "hate" ourselves and lash out at the world in an endless vicious cycle.

I put down the book. Seeking relief from these weighty thoughts, my mind drifts to Oshanta, how she so noiselessly moved through the woods. Even when she unearthed the handful of grass in her ritual to the four winds, there was no tearing sound, as when I did the same thing. Then, the grace with which she raised her hand and brought it to her heart. I begin to imagine what this graceful, lithe body might look like underneath the loose sweaters and long skirts she wears: beginning with her hands, the eyes of my imagination travel to her probably beautiful shoulders, then down her slightly arched like-a-dancer's back, then ... I stop myself. I feel voyeuristic, sinful—why? She's an attractive woman, yes, but ... what? Katherine, I haven't been with a woman since Katherine. During our 15 years together, I was never more than glancingly attracted to any other woman. Then pre-Katherine, there had been only a few unserious relationships.

Could it also be that what's making me hesitate is I've never known a woman of color, much less dated one? Though I don't consider myself at all racially bigoted, maybe deep down, I am. I remember a boy—George was his name—from the only black family in the town I grew up in. He was quiet and smart and knew a lot of answers to teachers' questions. I remember him always sitting in the back of the bus on the way to school in the 50s, and my sense of how unfair this seemed and how, despite my persistent invitations to him to come sit with me, he wouldn't. So I sat with him in the back, and all the other kids would turn around to stare, whispering to each other.

I gaze out at the ocean. If I want to be with Oshanta, then how should I go about it? Ask her out to dinner? But I have no desire to "go out." I could ask her to come here for dinner. But my cooking is so rudimentary. Really, who am I kidding? I wouldn't even know how to act on an actual date.

It's the day for Oshanta to come. I feel an excitement, a tingling to the tips of my fingers.

A knock; I open the door. Her face looks sad, even as if she'd been crying. "Hello, Oshanta. Is something wrong?"

"Yes, but I don't want to bother you with my problems." She takes off her orange and brown poncho and hangs it in the closet.

"You wouldn't be bothering me. Why don't we go in the living room here and talk."

We sit down. She looks at me with her beautiful burnt sienna eyes and takes a deep breath. "Yesterday I went for a walk, back to the Indian village you and I had visited. I was planning to take pictures for the photographic record I'm compiling for our case. As I was walking along the path, I heard a clanging sound that got louder the closer I came to the village. Then I heard a rumbling and the ground began to shake.

"I ran toward the sound. When I reached the edge of the village, the sound was deafening. Then, in the middle of the site, I saw a well-drilling machine and three hard-hatted men standing around watching this big steel rod plunge into the ground.

"I don't think I've ever been so astounded by anything I've seen. I'm glad I had my camera, for I had something useful to do with my anger. I ran out to the clearing and began to take pictures. The men saw me and one of them started coming toward me waving his hands and looking angry. It was clear he didn't like the idea of pictures being taken. I ran back into the woods. He stopped when he got to the edge and couldn't see me anymore.

"When I returned home, I immediately called the state park ranger's office to find out how such a thing could be happening in a public park. The ranger, whom I know from my walks in the park, said he was not aware of any such activity and would go right down there and then call me back when he knew more. About an hour later he called, very upset. He said he was still trying to reach the Long Island regional state parks commissioner, but that apparently a company was given permission to dig a test well for water in that part of the park. He said the men at the site claimed to have an agreement with the state, but didn't have a copy of it with them. They apologized for not informing the park ranger before they began their activity. When he asked what the drilling was for, they responded that it was to explore the possibility of building a golf course in the park and the amount of water in the ground was the first factor that had to be determined. The ranger told me he then asked them to stop their drilling until he found out more.

"I said they were drilling right in the middle of a valuable archaeological and sacred Montaukett Indian site and, in addition to it probably being illegal to do such a thing in a public park, it was an outrage to be doing it where they were. He said he understood how I would feel this way, and that he himself took visitors on hikes to the village site. As soon as he found out from his superiors exactly what was going on, he said he would let me know. He hasn't called me back yet, though this all happened at only about three o'clock yesterday afternoon." She sighs and shakes her head.

"What will you do?"

"I'm having my photographs developed and then am going to Albany to talk to some state legislators. There have been rumors for a while that the state, in its plans to privatize various public services in order to cut down on spending, might consider allowing some commercial enterprises in this and other parks."

"Yes, that seems to be a trend, in national parks as well, like Yosemite, parts of which are reportedly becoming littered with motels, fast food places and billboards."

"What's particularly galling is that this parkland was saved from development about 20 years ago by the state, the result of efforts by local concerned people to fight a luxury condominium resort plan and convince the state it was too ecologically valuable and sensitive to be destroyed. After the state bought the land, with taxpayers' money, its archaeological significance also began to be recognized. And now the government is abdicating its commitment to protect it by putting it back in the hands of developers.

"This new scheme, however, poses more of a threat, because I hear many local people are not opposed now to some sort of commercialization that would attract more tourists to the area. Golf being as popular as it is, it would definitely accomplish that. They also think a golf course wouldn't disturb the land as condominiums would.

"Whatever the particulars, it's all really the same story repeating itself: of power, greed, money, of government not living up to its obligations, of taking advantage of people perceived as powerless, of disrespect for history, for nature, for generations of the past and the future.

"So, as the spirits of my ancestors have decreed, I must be the voice for those stories—of the land, its history and people—others are unable or unwilling to hear."

Then Came the Men

Journal entry, November 18:
I called the office today. I felt an obligation to let Madeline know I'm still okay. She said people have been calling—Katherine and my parents especially—trying to find out what happened to me. She told them she'd heard from me and that I'm all right. The firm hired a young lawyer to fill in for me during my "psychologically necessary leave of absence," as she said she described my sudden departure. When she asked if I was in therapy, I responded not in a professional sense, but being alone and in the country was helping me more than any therapist probably could. She ended, almost tearfully, with "I hope you can find some happiness."

The telephone rings. No one other than Madeline and Oshanta knows my phone number.

"Paul, I hope you don't mind my calling you." Oshanta's voice, usually fluid and calm, is shaky. "I received what appears to be a threatening letter in my post office box this morning. This is what it says: 'Beware to those who seek to see. The surest way to protect the positives is to destroy the negatives.' It's postmarked from Montauk, yesterday. There's no signature, and it's typed from a computer."

"Why don't you come here and we'll talk about it."

I feel myself starting to get tense. I like Oshanta, but that doesn't mean I want to get involved in the complications of her life. She fit in so well in the beginning—like this view of the ocean, something beautiful to be contemplated and appreciated, but one doesn't need to plunge into its depths to …

The ocean of emotion that forever pounds at the bluffs of reason. And where, looking out as far as I can see across the water, do these waves of emotion actually begin?

A knock at the door. As I open it, I see Oshanta looks upset. I carefully put my arms around her. Her head falling below my chin, I feel her fast, warm breath through my shirt. After a moment, she gently releases herself from my embrace and hands me the note.

"Do you have any idea who wrote this?"

"This is only a guess, but it might be the man who chased me from the site the other day. I didn't recognize him at first, but afterwards I thought about it and I think he was Marshall Kincaid, a local builder, very successful, who also owns a restaurant in town where I met him once. He seemed quite nice. He talked about how his family went back four generations in this area, and that they once lived on the land that is now the state park. I said, playfully, not accusingly, so your ancestors might be the ones who took it from mine. But he took offense and suddenly the smile vanished, replaced by a glowering look.

"People in town who don't know him well also seem to think he's charming, but even if they don't, he brings jobs and money into town, and also donates money to many charities. Some say he's cheated them and lied to them. If he is involved with this golf course scheme and has the potential to make a lot of money, who knows how far he'd go to get what he wants. Then, there's also the incentive of, in some form, getting back what he sees as rightfully belonging to him. His proprietary feeling toward this land was made very clear when we met."

"Did his family own the land when the state bought it?"

"No, apparently his grandfather, the last to own it, went bankrupt. Then it was sold to a man who wanted to build condominiums on it, which is when the state stepped in."

"Well, I suppose the state can legally license a concessionaire to put in and run a golf course, but I'm sure they have to go through an environmental review before they approve such a major development. After all, although this is not my area of legal expertise, I do know that a golf course has a major impact on a water supply: the drain on the supply because of the irrigation required and the pesticides on the grass that can go into the groundwater."

"I did some looking into the groundwater status in that area of the park when, as I pointed out to you before, the streams that were once healthy were diminishing to a trickle. I learned that the soil here is not very deep, and has a porous, sandy base, which allows for easy pollutant contamination. The water table is also relatively thin, relying almost entirely on rain water to supply it, and therefore doesn't lend itself to development."

"So, if an environmental impact study were done, a golf course might not be permitted. First, we have to find out if any permits have been issued, then if they are allowed to drill a test well without an impact study, and also if there's an agreement of some kind with the state to do this project.

"I think the local newspapers should be informed about what's going on down there. The more public you make the matter the less likely the people involved will feel they can get away with acting improperly or illegally."

"I'll call a reporter I know from the local paper and, as soon as the pictures are developed, I'll give her one. Thanks for your help, Paul." She takes my hand in hers and squeezes it. "May I use the phone?"

"Of course."

In a moment she returns. "There was a message on my machine from the park ranger. He said he spoke to the park commissioner who verified that he does have a contract with a company, Out East Development, to dig a test well, but that there was an oversight on the contractor's part in obtaining the permit from the State Department of Environmental Conservation to do it. They have supposedly ceased their activity temporarily, which means they must have every intention of continuing. I'm going to see the ranger right now, and then I'm going to see the commissioner. This is truly unbelievable."

"I'll go with you."

"We'll go in my car."

When we walk in to the lobby area of the park ranger's building, we hear two men talking inside. We're looking at some maps of the park on the wall and hear one man say: "I don't want people going down to that part of the park now. Put some barriers and signs up. One that says 'Especially No Feisty Injuns Allowed.'" He laughs.

We turn to each other at the same time. I think I'm more shocked than Oshanta, for this might not be the first time she's heard a racial slur directed toward her, but it's the first time I've been with someone on the receiving end of one. It makes me feel sick to my stomach.

After a moment of silence and no other laughter, there's another voice.

"But commissioner, sir, with all due respect, this is a park. How can I keep people out? And I don't think it's advisable to be drilling right there. There're other places they could test. We could have some problems on our hands because of it."

"The natives will get restless, eh? Well, we'll fix everything. Don't you worry, Frank."

They walk in to the lobby. We stare at each other. No one seems to know what to say. The man whom I assume is the ranger because of his uniform rakes his hand through his hair and looks down at the floor, his head shifting from side to side. The commissioner is moving his mouth almost imperceptibly, groping for some words, the look of a man struggling to maintain a modicum of dignity in the face of embarrassment. But the embarrassment is only superficial, for the eyes aren't moving or changing a bit, just the mouth is. A stocky man, the commissioner visibly puffs himself up and his face takes on a kind of congenial glaze.

"Well, Frank, looks as if you have some visitors. Kind of brisk out there today, but a good day for a hearty hike." He turns to Frank and shakes his hand. "I've got to run off. Good to see you, Frank." He starts to walk toward the door.

"Just a moment, sir," Oshanta calls after him. "Are you the park commissioner?"

"Yes, yes I am."

"My name is Mariah Pharaoh. I'm a native of Montauk, in both senses of the word. I was born and raised here and am of Montauk Native American descent. I'm not here to go for a pleasant hike today. I'm here because of what I was shocked to discover on what was supposed to be a pleasant hike the other day. I'm referring to the drilling going on in the park in Indian Fields. I informed Mr.

Fithian here, who said he would find out what he could and get back to me. I understand the company has permission to do the drilling and has only ceased while waiting for a D.E.C. permit. Is this correct?"

"Why yes, Miss Pharaoh. We're trying to find out the water situation in the park. It's something we've long planned to do, frankly. The company we contracted with made a slight error in forgetting to get all the paperwork done." He laughs. "The bureaucracy—can't get around it. I should know—hah—a pain in the-you-know-what sometimes. They also kind of misjudged where to dig the test well. They weren't supposed to do it there, but because it's one of the few areas clear of brush, and not as hard to get to as some others, they chose to do it there. They were also getting a little anxious to do it before the winter set in and the ground started to freeze."

"Commissioner, number one, they are drilling in a historic Montauk Indian village; and number two, an environmental impact study would probably be required before any drilling is done."

"You're wrong on number two there, Miss Pharaoh. Because it's state park land, we don't need an EIS just for a test well. And as to number one, well, I know it's a historic site—though you probably know that it has not yet been officially designated as such—but it's just a test well, and they'll put everything back just as it was when they're finished."

"Finished, you mean finished building the golf course?"

The commissioner shoots a surprised look at Frank. "Well, that's just an idea floating around, Miss Pharaoh, nothing written in stone. Not a bad idea though. Would make a terrific golf course, really—natural rolling hills, big fields that easily lend themselves to fairways. I get excited just thinking about it. Golf is such a great game. Don't you agree, Miss?"

Oshanta stares silently at him in disbelief.

"No, I'm afraid I don't share your enthusiasm. In fact, I despise the idea. And I won't sit idly by while this assault takes place on this beautiful piece of land that belongs to the taxpayers of New York, though originally, and possibly still, to my people, both of whom should and will have a say in this matter. I assure you, commissioner, the natives will get restless. Good day, Mr. Fithian."

I cannot suppress the smile coming over my face: such passion yet control, strength and clarity.

"Oshanta, you're going to make a great lawyer."

How a Flicker Becomes a Flame

I've been staring at this blank piece of paper for a while. I've got an idea for a story, but just can't begin. It's not so much a matter of finding the right words, or a fear of whether it will be "good" or not. Writing in my journal and some occasional poems has given me a degree of confidence at least to attempt a story. But neither seems to carry the same weight of purposefulness as writing a story does. So this block is more an existential fear: a voice saying that what I'm going to write really has no purpose, just words on a page that reflect something real only to me and of use, if at all, only to me. And if this is so, is that reason enough to write?

This voice of doubt doesn't surprise me, considering the utilitarian nature of the legal writing I'm accustomed to. Well, who knows? Maybe a story I will write could benefit someone beyond me. However, though it seems like a paradox, any kind of purposefulness, beyond trying to understand some questions by putting words together in a pleasing way, becomes inhibiting.

Maybe now I can begin.

> George rocked slowly back and forth in the old oak rocker as he gazed into the fire that had now died down to a core of glowing embers. Druid, his dog, lay next to him, also gazing fixedly into the fire. What was it about a fire that held the attention so?

Perhaps, George thought, it sparked in us a distant dark memory of gazing into a fire when fire was nothing less than the profoundest miracle, our first giant step forward in controlling an otherwise strange and hostile universe. Yes, fires might remind us, however dimly, of this, but fires seem to evoke a more immediate memory, George reflected; not of any particular event or image, rather of a vague feeling or spirit, of a life he had once imagined living that somehow had never come to be.

Startled by this thought, George suddenly stopped rocking. Ever alert to the slightest shift in his master's movements or moods, Druid lifted his head from the floor and looked inquisitively at George. He knew when his master was sad, as well as when he was happy.

I look up from the page into the stone fireplace. Wow! I feel like I've just been on an exciting adventure—adrenalin rushing through me, brain cells rapidly firing—and discovered some new, exotic place, though it was just an adventure in my head and a discovery of a mental place, a deeper dimension, from which to view the world. And a realization that—my God, this place was always here! I also feel like kind of magician, having made something with form, substance and life, however amateurish, out of nothing, out of mere thought and imagination.

I read it over and over, the euphoric high subsiding as I focus my mind more on the style and content. A little stiff and too abstract, not alive enough, but there is some life in it, some feel of real. As I think about George, however, an eerie feeling starts to creep over me; the picture I'm seeing looks more and more like—me! And I hadn't intended to write about myself at all! A chill shivers through me. I stare into the empty, gaping fireplace: *"... of a life he had once imagined living but somehow had never come to be."*

My thoughts flick frantically backwards, searching through the ashes. An image of Katherine leaps before me: she, in one of the law school classes we took together, sitting in front of me with a gracefulness that belied the discomfort of the wooden desk chair, her head slightly tilted to the right, golden hair falling over her shoulder; my almost overwhelming desire to put my hand gently on her left shoulder and my lips near her ear and whisper, "I want only you."

I see myself at the firm, the mahogany desk and bookshelves lining the walls lending the room an insular dignity and security. What about my desire to become a senior partner and then go on to be a judge? But these weren't burning desires, dim goals at best. The passion I had for my profession in the beginning had begun to wane early on.

My marriage? Yes, there was passion but when that, too, began to wane, the desire to have a child was something I imagined, though not always consciously, would have been the breath of air to ignite passion again, in my marriage and my life; my life that somehow, without my knowing why—how does this happen, how does someone lose sight of his own life?—had dwindled to a steady, uninspired flicker. Amidst the ashes, I see a child growing inside of Katherine.

Panic rushes through my body, my brain. A voice says, there's nothing you can do about the thing that's hurting you so, that won't go away, no matter how far you go, how much you try to change your life, yourself.

I bolt up, throw my pen into the fireplace, then pages of the spiral-bound notebook, tearing them out, crumbling them in a ball. "This is all bullshit! This whole damn thing I'm trying to do out here," I say out loud.

I look wildly around me. I want to smash something, cause it to break into pieces. I see a beautiful vase on a table. Something stops me. I look at the notebook paper in the fireplace. I find some matches. Watch the flames begin to rise. Paper goes up so fast: words, histories, stories, lives—pouf and they're gone.

I'm calming down watching the fire, the fire drawing me in, now dying down to a few blackened pages with burning orange edges. This reminds me of something, but I can't quite retrieve it. Yes: the image of me as a boy, like a bright shining star inside the dark body of me as a man, that revelatory moment on the bluff my first night in Montauk; then how that bright shining boy began to grow out to the edges of the dark surrounding image until he filled it completely.

The glowing edges in the fireplace fade and the blackened paper shrivels, reduced to only a few ashes. So this is the end, of the story I was trying to write, the story I was trying to live: unfinished stories, with perhaps some promise but not enough—desire to see them through? Or is it that the desire itself is not right and that I just thought in my desperation I needed this much change? What in God's name is it I really need?

My hands clasp in desperate prayer. Staring at them, I remember how fervently I prayed as a child before going to bed. After the "Now I lay me down to sleep I pray the Lord my soul to keep ..." and blessing everyone I loved, I would ask God two things: to help me be a better person and to help me know what it was I was supposed to do with my life. Incredible! Thirty-odd years later I'm still asking God what I should do with my life, though now it's a different kind of asking. Then I was trying to know what to be: a lawyer, as my Dad wanted, a priest, as I felt inclined to be, or a writer, as my romantic mother seemed to think I should be. Now the choices are not from out there but inside; not so much *what* to be but *how*.

And what about the better person wish? Have I been kind, thoughtful, giving—to Katherine, to my parents, to anyone?

My fingers twine more tightly together, my eyes squeeze shut. No, never enough, to anyone, and maybe most of all— "to me," I say out loud.

I open my eyes, surprised, as if someone else were speaking, look into the fireplace and the smoldering ashes.

Perhaps, with a little patience and forgiveness, I can feed the fire inside and make the flicker become a flame.

Dune Sunset

What is it about a walk in a beautiful place that helps so to clear the mind? On this autumnal afternoon, the sky is already beginning to dim, the quantity of light receding as the darkness of winter grows ever closer. The most prevalent plant in this landscape, the shad bush (a name which I learned from Oshanta), its leaves a passionate deep purple-red a few weeks ago, is now nearly leafless. I think of what it will look like in the spring when, as Oshanta also informed me, they form a vast panorama of antique white flowers so spectacular people come to sightsee them. I wonder if I'll still be here then.

    I follow the short path that leads down to the beach. Off to the west along the edge of the bluffs is a narrow and well-trodden trail I've not yet taken. To the south is a steep drop to the beach and to the north, thick brush.

    A tern darts by me, headed out to sea, such a sparkling creature skimming with zest and precision just above the vast, titanic ocean. Although I know it's a tern, I note its markings and size, to determine later what kind. I'm learning more about birds since being here, studying them with my binoculars and a guide book I bought, something that interested me as a child. The thrill I feel in seeing this bird and knowing its name, at least in part, seems nearly the same I felt as a child.

Nature can put us in touch with a place in ourselves where no barriers of time exist. Stopping, I turn my face toward the sky, close my eyes for a moment, feel the sun and wind upon my face, breathe in the sea air.

Ahead I see the path turns away from the edge into a kind of dwarf forest, windswept trees no taller than me creating a canopy over the trail. As I enter I realize they aren't trees but shad bushes; I didn't know they could grow so tall. Their trunks are turning an almost iridescent silver color which shimmers when struck by a shaft of light. Some say this is why the plant is so named, Oshanta told me: at this time of year its color resembles the silvery shad fish that once ran seasonally in these waters. Shad also has an edible berry, once prized by the Montauks who introduced it to the settlers who began to call it "service berry," because it would ripen in June when ministers would travel to the towns to bury those who died during the winter but could not be interred until the ground had finally thawed.

The growth of the shad is so lush and dense, I feel as if I'm caught in an intricate, lovely web made of lace. A paradoxical sense of being sheltered and, at the same time, on the verge of being lost in a labyrinth I might not be able to find my way out of, comes over me. I strain in vain to see ahead, for the path twists and turns like an old gnarled tree. Muscles in my legs tense with a slight twinge of fear, or is it more excitement than fear?

Fear of what they don't know and of their emotions that, like the ocean, forever pound at their bluffs of reason. I stop and look up through small openings in the canopy of branches, see clouds passing high above in a pale blue sky. Opening up yourself to not knowing: is this what feeding the fire inside is?

I have the uncanny sense I'm seeing blue sky, seeing trees and leaves for the first time. I reach out to touch a branch and imagine I can feel the life coursing through it.

As I walk ahead a few feet, the forest abruptly ends and a vast, moonlike landscape begins, of cratered dunes dotted with tufts of dune grass on their wavelike crests and occasional dwarf windswept pines. Coming from the deep shade of the forest, I squint from the sudden comparative brightness of the waning sun upon almost pure white sand.

What a strange and other-worldly place! In the middle of a huge hollow, I'm engulfed by its diameter and the height of the rising dune to the east. From the little I know of geology, these dunes were formed by a glacier deposited here 15,000 years ago. Yet, these dunes are different from others I've seen. So like the shapes of great waves, even with a little curl at the top of their faces which must be about 20 feet high, perhaps these dunes were also formed by the forces of wind and waves.

I remember my walk with Oshanta to Indian Fields and the voices of her ancestors speaking to her. Are there voices that might speak to me, here in this enchanted place? Voices that might tell me what mission in life I'm meant to fulfill? Shall I take a handful of sand and toss it to the four winds to see if they'll answer me? I pick up a handful, let it sift through my fingers. I close my eyes and listen: the sound of the surf, pounding in the distance, echoes off the face of the dune, and the wind whispers over the crest of grass above. I feel a lightness, a freedom from thought standing in the center of this ancient dune, grains of sand older than man whirling in the wind, the sinking sun shining its last rays of the day upon my face.

On the northwest edge of my awareness, I think I hear something, then realize it's not something I hear but sense in another way. Opening my eyes, I turn around, and there, coming toward me from the north, is Oshanta. In this no-man's land where senses of time and place have ceased, she's like an apparition a wanderer imagines he sees after traveling many miles across desert sand. I blink hard twice. She comes closer. It appears as if she's floating a few feet above the sand, her long black hair and a scarf waving in the wind. We're only a few feet away from each other now. She's looking as incredulously at me, I think, as I am at her. Words—they're escaping me, like the wind, like the rays of the orange setting sun. The only thing I can say is her name.

"Paul," she says, smiling, touching my hand lightly with hers. "What a surprise. This is one of my favorite places to walk, especially at this time of year when the sunset is so spectacular. Let's move over here, out of the dune, so we can see it better."

The clouds along the horizon are a deep purple-gray, the sun becoming a brighter orange by the moment. I want only to enjoy the moment, but I can't help wonder how I'll find my way out of here once the sun is gone.

As if reading my thoughts, Oshanta says, "Don't worry about the darkness. Look over there." I look back toward the east. An almost full moon is rising in the sky.

"Besides, I could probably find my way blindfolded in here." She taps my hand again lightly with her fingers. Before she can take them away, I capture them, entwine them in mine.

The setting sun is now at its peak of intensity, a huge burning ember in the sky just before it begins to die. Our palms feel as if they're burning, spreading the flame, feeding the fire inside.

Aunt Olivia and the Thunderbird Stone

Journal entry, November 20:
I don't want to say too much; words could take the magic away. It has been that so singular kind of day when life seems filled with—it's here, in this meeting place of heart, mind and spirit that language is so wanting—what perhaps can't be better expressed than with the word grace.

I wish it never had to end. But I can't stay awake any longer.

I'm walking down a city street, skyscrapers rising on both sides. It's cold and blustery. I bow my head and pull up the collar on my coat. The wind is so strong, I feel as if I'm almost not moving forward at all.

There's no one else in sight, no cars or buses, and no sounds except for the wind. I'm getting colder and wearier. I lift my head to see how far I have to go to the end of the street. I decide I must retreat somewhere out of the wind, to rest and get warm. Off to the left is a narrow street, not wide enough for cars, where about halfway down I see a bonfire burning. I walk hurriedly toward it.

It's a very large fire, the flames leaping about a foot above my head. As I stand there, the warmth spreading throughout my body, I look into the heart of the fire. I see a photograph of Katherine framed in deep red leather, its edges burning. I see tears forming in her eyes. She moves her mouth. I can't hear what she's saying, but read her lips to be saying, "You must feed the fire or the fire will die. I'm sorry I never told you this. I'll always love you. Goodbye."

I thrust my hand into the fire. The flames, strangely, don't burn me. But to reach Katherine's picture, I must plunge my whole self into the fire. Even though I know now I won't be burned, I'm too afraid. A sudden strong wind comes down the alleyway. Looking up, I see, just above the tall buildings, the face of Oshanta Runs with the Wind, her mouth pursed as if she's creating the wind. The flames rise even higher. She speaks to me:

Don't be afraid.
We come to tear away the veil.
Unlike the shining sun that makes you smile and feel content,
the wind alone unravels you,
filling you with fear
of the wide emptiness now you feel so near.
You must listen to these ghosts
that howl and swirl around you,
voices of the past and of the future
threatening to consume you.
You must walk through them, let them burn you if they may,
But do not, do not run away.

I walk into the fire, reach for the photograph. But just as I touch it, it turns to ashes.

I awake with a start. I know I've had a powerful dream, but it's gone. Closing my eyes, I try to remember it, but nothing comes. The sun is just beginning to rise. I look in the mirror and see what appear to be tears in my eyes.

Yes—the photograph of Katherine with tears in her eyes, burning in the fire on a cold and windy city street; and her words to me—"Feed the fire or the fire will die. I'm sorry I never told you this."

The alarm clock rings, startling me. Oshanta is coming soon to take me to meet her great aunt Olivia Pharaoh, but I'll quickly write down this dream in my journal so I won't forget it.

A knock at the door. "Hello, Oshanta. I'm ready, but still sort of waking up. I had quite a dream last night." I shake my head. "It's strange. I never used to dream much before. Perhaps it has something to do with being out here."

We start walking toward her car. "I've been keeping a journal of my dreams for a long time," she says. "I see them as sort of interior snapshots, pictures of my life, distilled and compressed. They bring things to the surface I'm not aware of. I think native peoples have traditionally been connected to their dream lives, seeing them as a powerful source of imagination. Native American seers, like Sitting Bull and Black Elk, could bridge the waking and dream worlds which gave their words great clarity and poetic power. My great aunt, you'll see, speaks very much in this way."

We're driving across the Napeague stretch, a thin spit of sandy land with the ocean to the south and Napeague Harbor and Gardiner's Bay to the north that separates Montauk from the rest of the South Fork.

"Napeague Harbor was once very rich in clams and scallops. Now they're so scarce that the town of East Hampton has been conducting a reseeding program to try to bring them back. It also used to be rich in menhaden, small herring-like fish that were processed for oil and to fertilize the fields." Oshanta points toward the east side of the harbor. "There was a fish processing factory along that side of the harbor, known as the Promised Land, which was, according to historians, a tongue-in-cheek name because rather than a land of milk and honey, it was a land of foul-smelling fish. However, it was a Promised Land in the sense that many people, from far and near, found employment there."

We drive off Cranberry Hole Road onto a narrow sandy road called Pharaoh's Landing, at the end of which we come to a group of small wooden cabins. Pointing to the one on the right, Oshanta says, "That's where I live." We walk up to the one in the middle. Oshanta knocks on the door and then opens it. "It's me, Oshanta, Aunt Olivia." Sitting in a rocking chair in front of the fireplace is a slight woman, her hair braided in a neat crown on her head and a shawl around her shoulders.

"Come in, my dear."

We walk toward her. "I brought a new friend for you to meet. This is Paul Collins, Paul, Olivia Pharaoh."

Her face, reflected in the firelight, is a fascinating mix of calmness yet intensity, sadness and happiness. Despite her elderly age, there's youthfulness, too, in her surprisingly smooth, light copper-colored skin and large dark eyes that dance like the flames of the fire. She extends her hand.

"Paul Collins. That's a nice name. Please sit down." Her voice is lively, lyrical. "I've made some tea for us, Oshanta. Would you bring it here? I'm afraid my ancient bones aren't being good to me today. I was out too long in the weather yesterday, picking cranberries for Thanksgiving: they're just at their peak and I felt a frost coming on last night. I can feel that in my bones, too—at least there's something good about getting this old!"

Her whole face smiles, not just her mouth, and radiates a warmth I can almost feel. I turn my gaze toward the fireplace. Katherine's words from my dream echo loudly in my mind: *Feed the fire or the fire will die. I'm sorry I never told you this.* There's a key here, in this paradox of opposites in Olivia's face and in fire itself: feeding the fire is not only something active, exciting, but something soothing and comforting; a metaphor for whatever creates a feeling of calmness and trust between two people, which perhaps has to do with simply listening, not only to what the other is saying but also to what she is not saying.

I bring my attention back to Oshanta and her aunt who are looking at me patiently. "Would you like your tea now?" Oshanta asks.

I take the cup from her. "Thank you. Forgive me for being rude. The fire just reminded me of something, a dream I've been thinking about."

"We could see you were thinking about something important. It would have been rude of us to interrupt you," Olivia says.

How unusual for people, particularly those I've only just met, to allow such a private moment to occur so naturally.

"I think fire reminds us of many things: of what we know and feel that burns deeply inside us, of what we do not know that remains just out of reach, and that reaching out to know more is what keeps us alive; and of the ever-present contradictions in life—of light and dark, creation and destruction. Important decisions were always made around a fire by my forefathers. Fire would help them see clearly, and to see something clearly, one must see its contradictions. See the brightness and light in the flames and darkness in the ashes? See how the flames dance, ever moving, reaching out to touch the air? Now, at this far point in my journey, I contemplate more the meaning of the glowing embers, try to become like a glowing ember in the fire of life."

Olivia smiles. "Of course, that is not easy when this ancient carcass acts up." Her expression changes quickly. "Or when men do bad things that make your flames of anger burn so you can hardly stand it. But we will fight them, right my brave one, Runs with the Wind?"

"Yes, we will. I would like to have your permission, as the elder of our people, to go to the state capital and plead our case. I brought these pictures for you to see, if you wish, what I described to you on the phone is happening in the Montauks' village." Olivia looks at them. Oshanta passes some to me.

"Has this stopped?" Olivia asks.

"For the time being. I went down there the other day with a reporter from the local paper, and the machine and the men were not there. Just the big hole in the ground and the tractor tracks through the woods."

Olivia takes a deep breath and stares into the fire. "Would you go over to the mantle and get a small stone there and bring it to me?" Oshanta brings back the stone and gives it to her aunt. She carefully rubs it with her fingers.

"This stone was handed down from our great sachem Wyandanch, then eventually to Stephen Pharaoh, then to King David, my grandfather, and, upon his death, to his wife, Queen Maria, then to her daughter Pocahontas, my mother, who gave it to me. I think now it is time for me to pass it on. The figure you see carved on it is the great Thunderbird. The fire of his eye and the thunder of his wings you need for your battle, and his wisdom as your guide. Keep it with you. Deep within its now smooth edges, held and carried by your ancestors on their sad marches off their land, in their futile battles in black-robed judges' courts, lies great power to help you on your journey." She places it in Oshanta's palm. The Thunderbird's eye dances in the light of the fire.

Bertrand

Oshanta and I walk out to the shore in front of the house. Such a beautiful shape to this body of water, Napeague Harbor. Almost a perfect U, it's about a quarter of a mile across and a half mile long before it opens into Gardiner's Bay directly north. The water is very still. A languid, lagoon-like feeling pervades, protected as it is by the encircling arms of the shoreline and, on the eastern side, by a rolling span of dunes—the Walking Dunes, Oshanta tells me.

"Exposed to the fierce northeast winter winds, the dunes are constantly shifting, thus their name. It's interesting how different this way of naming is from the way Native Americans traditionally named places after the natural features to be found there, like Napeague, which in Montaukett means 'water land'; and the way they would name themselves after something found in nature, imposing upon their identities the features of the natural world, not the other way around."

"Like Oshanta Runs with the Wind."

"If you could be named after something in nature, what would you choose?"

"That would be hard to say. Central Park has been pretty much the extent of my connection with nature for most of my adult life, and even as beautiful an oasis as it is, it's still not quite 'nature' like this cove and these dunes. But if I had to choose a name for myself now, it might be Paul Listens to the Ocean, because that's actually what I spend a lot of time doing." She turns her head toward me and smiles.

Up ahead a man is clamming offshore. Standing perfectly balanced in his boat, he carefully rakes the bottomland.

"In a way, I envy that clammer out there because he probably doesn't 'think' about, in an abstract way as I am, how he is connected to nature, this water: its meaning and mystery are part of him, who he is. But, maybe he's missing something too, by not pondering such things."

We stop walking as Oshanta looks intently at the clammer. "Perhaps we shouldn't think in terms of either/or, for it only limits us. That clammer is a perfect example. I'm quite sure he's my cousin Bertrand, Olivia's grandson, and with him it's not a question of being either clammer or thinker: he's both."

I feel chastened, though there's no hint of chastising in Oshanta's voice. "Bertrand—that's a name I don't hear very often. Does he also have a Montauk name?"

"His parents distanced themselves as much as possible from their Native American heritage, so they picked a name that's about as foreign as you can get. Bertrand's father, Olivia's son, was mostly Montaukett with some Shinnecock blood, and his mother was one half Montauk and the other half Caucasian. Because the Montauk tribe in this area dwindled to so few people, we were forced to intermarry with the Shinnecocks in Southampton and the small black population that was here; then, later, there was some limited intermarrying with the whites.

"The question of what we are, what heritage to identify with, is a wrenching question for all of us, because we all are of mixed blood now. Aunt Olivia is the only one left here who is a full-blooded Montauk. I'm about three-quarters Montauk and the rest Caucasian and African American. This matter of blood has caused too much divisiveness among us. Just as Judge Blackmar tried to deny there were Montauks in his courtroom in 1909, based on what he presumed to be their lesser amount of Montauk than African American, Shinnecock or white blood, and because every time a Montaukett would die, newspapers would report so-and-so was the 'last of the Montauks,' we discriminate against each other for the same reasons. And, of course, many of us try to deny our

Native American heritage altogether choosing instead to identify with white society.

"As for me, I've finally come to accept and like all the ethnic parts of me. And so has Bertrand. If anything, he identifies more with his Native Americanness now, I think in some way to compensate for what he sees as his parents' betrayal to their heritage. Actually, he was thinking of changing his name until he discovered the philosopher Bertrand Russell in college and decided he'd keep it after all."

Standing on the shoreline, Oshanta waves to him. After a few moments, he waves back and starts to row to shore. His strokes are even, deep and soundless; his boat undulates through the water. It's a powerful sight, this man and his vessel, as if painted with the same palette and brush strokes as the sea and the sky.

The boat reaches the shore and Bertrand deftly leaps out and walks toward us.

Despite the cumbersome black rubber wading boots he's wearing, his stride is long and graceful. I can see his startling blue-green eyes even from this far away, which seem to become greener as the water recedes behind him and he approaches the seaweeded shoreline. His skin is lighter than Oshanta's light reddish brown and his black hair is curly rather than straight. The late morning sun at his back etches his figure in light, recalling the first time I saw Oshanta silhouetted by the sunlight in the doorway of the room at the Memory Motel. The power of her presence then was not unlike this man's now, appearing like some kind of god arising full-blown out of the watery depths.

"Bertrand, how good to see you. It's been too long." Oshanta gives him a hug and a kiss.

"Yes, it has. I miss my favorite place in the world—and my favorite people. I've just not been able to free myself of my city chains lately. I've been teaching a painting class, in addition to my regular free-lance work. But I'm planning to spend some time here now, preparing for a show I'm having next month. Today, though, I decided I needed to get out and stick my feet in the mud for a while." He smiles like a gleeful child.

"Bertrand, this is Paul Collins. He just escaped from the city, too."

"Congratulations! You picked the right time of year. The bluefish are running, the clamming is good, the surf is the best, the sunsets the grandest and the people have gone. What more could you ask for?"

"You certainly looked very much in your element out there," I say.

"I worked as a bayman for many a season before and during college. This is so much a part of me," he says as he turns and waves his arm following the shape of the harbor, "that I need to literally touch it to feel whole again. When you live in the city, surrounded by manmade everything, it's easy to lose a proper perspective—what one of my favorite philosophers, Bertrand Russell, called the danger of our 'cosmic impiety.'"

"Yes, I remember that phrase—I was a philosophy major. My friends and I were much taken with Dewey, and before him, Nietzsche."

"The 'power philosophers' as Russell called them. Well, I think Russell is proving to be more right than ever. Our belief in our limitless power is what's gotten us into such a terrible mess today: we've lost our humility."

"That's really interesting, because I've just been re-reading Nietzsche, and I'm amazed at how differently I react to him now. It seems to me we're not even aware of how attractive and intoxicating this sense of power can be; and to keep it in check takes real effort—or sometimes perhaps the experience of deep loss."

Then, as if the three of us standing together on the shore hear the same voice calling out from the distant fog to where the sea and sky meet, we turn our gazes silently toward that vanishing point.

It's the first time I've said or thought those words—deep loss—since leaving everything and coming here. A sudden pain grips my heart, but almost as quickly, it lets go: maybe it's the passing of time, the experience of being with others who seem to understand, or maybe it's just the fog and the sky and the sea comforting me.

Oshanta turns to Bertrand. "Will you invite us to your studio, to see what you're working on?"

He hesitates. "I'm almost finished with one large canvas, then I'd love to have you come by."

"Great. See you Thanksgiving." She kisses him on the cheek. I shake his hand: strong yet sensitive, a hand that vigorously, carefully works the bottom of these waters and, I imagine, just as vigorously and carefully paints these same waters to life. He smiles, like the bright sun suddenly breaking through a foggy sky.

The Coyote

"I'm leaving for Albany this afternoon. Would you like to have some lunch in town before I go?" Oshanta asks as we arrive back at her great aunt's house and get in the car.

"Sure."

"Oh, and forgive me for forgetting to invite you before, but I hope you'll join us for Thanksgiving."

I hadn't even thought about Thanksgiving until Oshanta's Aunt Olivia mentioned it this morning. Now that I think about it, I can't recall a Thanksgiving when I wasn't with my parents: sitting around their dining room table, Father carving the turkey as Mother looked on admiringly, dwelling on each subtle slice of the knife, and with one of the most contented expressions I ever detected in her. I imagined this was because carving the Thanksgiving turkey was the one occasion in the year she felt Father truly became part of her world—the home, the family—the one day out of all the 360 when a more or less pure spirit of domestic harmony prevailed. When Katherine joined the family, this spirit became stronger, for my parents treated Katherine more as the daughter they never had than as a daughter-in-law.

"Thank you, Oshanta. Are you sure it won't be an imposition? After all, I just met your great aunt and cousin, and, though it doesn't seem so, I've only known you for a short time, too."

"I'm sure. I think Thanksgiving might be different for us than for you. It's a more communal event, the way it was celebrated originally by our people, as a ritual thanks for the fall harvest of the crops planted at Indian Fields. It was our most important celebration, the next most important being the spring planting. These were our versions of religious holidays."

We pull up in front of a restaurant. "Let's stop here for lunch. It's one of only two restaurants open for lunch at this time of year. It's Marshall Kincaid's, the fellow I think is involved with the golf course plan, but he's rarely here at this time of day."

We sit down at a table. Rustic fishing décor—nets, spears and other tools of the trade—along with large black and white photographs of Montauk in times past, adorn the dark wood walls. Above our seat is an aerial photo of a mostly wooded peninsula broken in a few places by expansive fields and a smattering of discernable structures: a farmhouse on the northern edge, two grand houses in the southern portion, a lighthouse at the eastern edge where the land ends and the ocean begins, and a bit to its southwest, a huge radar tower with some bunker-like buildings tucked in to the landscape.

"This is where I like to sit when I come here, because that photo is of the area where the Montauks once lived; the northern portion is where the village we walked to is. The farmhouse is the park building we were in where we met the park ranger and commissioner. The southern section, where the Montauks also once lived, is where your house is. The large fields are where the cattle grazed."

"When were these taken?"

"In the early 1950s. And, though there are certainly more houses now, most of the land remains as you see it here, preserved as it was beginning in the '50s as state and county parkland."

Three men come in the room and sit down at the booth behind ours. One of them I recognize as the park commissioner we met. Another one is reading a newspaper.

"Look at these damn pictures. And this goddamn headline: Drilling in Montauks' Ancestral Village. Don't you just hate it when newspapers stick their noses into stuff and go off half-cocked, inflaming everyone for no reason?"

The Last Resort

"And all because of that prying, pain-in-the-ass Indian," the commissioner says. Oshanta, who has her back toward them and didn't see them come in, appears to have turned a shade paler.

"It's the park commissioner, as you probably guessed, with two other men," I whisper.

"I bet one of them is Marshall Kincaid. The local newspaper has just come out. I like the headline." She smiles. "What does the fellow who's reading the newspaper look like?"

"He's kind of ruggedly handsome, square jaw, blondish hair and blue-grey eyes. Looks pretty mean at the moment."

"That sounds like Marshall Kincaid. People around here nicknamed him the Coyote, which is interesting since the Coyote is an important figure in Native American mythologies. Also known as the Trickster, the Coyote is cunning, deceptive and charming. He can change shape and identity, so as soon as we think we recognize him, he becomes something else. In Native American stories he is equally good and bad, capable of greed and pride, but also of kindness and generosity. The latter attributes, however, usually appear toward the end of the stories."

"So, there might be hope this Marshall Kincaid will see the light at the end of the story?" I whisper.

"We shall see."

We get up to leave, and as we walk by Mr. Kincaid's table, he looks up and recognizes Oshanta. He appears momentarily aghast. We keep walking, but then he says, "Hi, Mariah is it?"

"Yes."

"I remember. We met right here, didn't we?"

"Yes, we did."

"And you were the one who came down the other day to the site in the park. Sorry about scaring you away. I thought you were just some nosy newspaper person. Listen, we were just checking out the water situation, at the commissioner's request. But, we've finished. We're gone. No water there, so don't worry. There's nothing anyone can do down there, right commissioner?"

"That's right. No water, end of story. Would have made a great golf course, but I know you don't agree with me about that, Miss."

"So, everything is right back the way it was before down there. Okay? No hard feelings?"

"I'll just have to find out for myself, thanks. Good day."

Outside, I ask Oshanta, "What do you think?"

"I don't have time to go down there now. I have to go to Albany, to do some research on the Montauks at the State Museum for purposes of our tribal recognition. I also have meetings scheduled with our Assemblyman and State Senator, to obtain letters of support for our case to the Federal Bureau of Indian Affairs."

"The Coyote is well nicknamed; a very smooth character indeed."

"I don't believe him. He was just too obsequious. And I know how he feels about that land. He won't give up so easily."

"He and the commissioner are definitely two of a kind."

"Yes, but the commissioner is only dangerous because of his position of power. Marshall is more dangerous because he's the one with the ideas, the passion and the money. I don't think the commissioner would be doing this without him."

"Well, together they may be a formidable opponent, but not more formidable than you—or certainly than us."

To See a Rhino in the Wild

*D*ruid walked over to his master and, with the sad, deeply sympathetic look one's best human friend couldn't equal, gave him a big lick on his cheek. Still staring into the fire, George put his hand upon Druid's head, stroking back behind the ears. Raising his gray-whiskered snout, Druid seemed to smile.

"What do you think, old boy? Worried 'bout me going a little batty in my old age, huh? Well, a man shouldn't let himself drift off like that too much. No, no, it's just not good. Got to always keep busy, focused, right? No good thinkin' too much, 'specially at my age—what difference would it make anyhow? Come on, lets you and me go for a nice walk, okay?"

Now "walk" was probably the second most important word to Druid, "food" being the first. But, strangely, instead of wagging his tail—so hard it usually made his entire body wag—he cocked his head, as if to say "Are you sure?"

George had always talked out loud to Druid, almost as if he were human, but since Helen died, he talked to him even more.

"Oh, so you'd rather stay here by the warm fire, is that it? The winters are gettin' too much for your old bones? Or maybe you don't think it's so bad lettin' your thoughts wander off, staring into the fire?"

As if understanding what his master was saying, Druid turned his head toward the fire.

I read over what I've just written. Not bad, considering this is the first time I've picked up writing this story since the day I thought I'd ended it in a fiery blaze. I can feel it more—there's more tone, texture, rhythm. A fascinating process, writing: how you first approach it—all cerebral, conceptual, language as pure intellect. And then you let the themes, words and images sink down from that lofty place, down into the rest of your body, into your chest where you breathe them and let them enter your heart, to your fingertips where you touch them and feel their shape, to your mouth where you roll them around, taste them. Making all art is perhaps something like this, but more difficult with writing, I suspect, because language is one step removed, a symbol rather than the immediate, sensory experience itself. Compared to playing a note on my trumpet, there's more alchemy required to transform this word, this phrase on this page into something someone else can feel in his fingertips and his heart.

I remember how Katherine would read poetry to me in the first years of our marriage, on quiet Sunday afternoons or late at night before going to sleep. Her favorites were Wordsworth and Yeats. Besides being an intellectual experience, it was a sensual one, too: listening to their words that almost sounded like songs, especially those of Yeats, in her voice that would begin in a strong, earthy and resonant tone and then gradually fade, suffused with a melancholy, wistful sound. This faltering was sometimes attributable to the mood of the poem itself, but I found other times it was more something in Katherine, something I didn't understand and that made me feel uneasy but was unable to talk to her about.

Voices of the past and of the future that howl and swirl around you ... but do not, do not run away. And Katherine's words from my dream of the fire: *Feed the fire or the fire will die. I'm sorry I never told you this.*

Maybe if I could learn to listen to that silent sadness between the sounds, that loneliness that separates us, I would see that it's also something that can connect us. I pick up my pen again.

The Last Resort

> "Okay, so I guess you're trying to tell me something. You win. We'll linger here by the fire a little longer."
>
> George sat back in the rocking chair and slowly stroked Druid's head. The embers still glowed, and a medium-sized birch log received a wandering spark and suddenly caught fire. The thought he had left—"...of a life I'd imagined living but somehow had never come to be"—rekindled in his mind.
>
> "What was that life? A life traveling the world, preferably by boat, with Helen, yes; I was going to retire at 55, then 60, 62, but then, of course, I didn't. Kept going, afraid to stop, I guess, afraid of...not knowing what to do, maybe, time just stretchin' out endlessly ahead of me. But I did know, just seemed kinda' scary.
>
> "Then, then Helen got sick. Maybe she'd just gotten tired of waiting for me. But she never said anything. She never told me 'George, damn it, let's get on the road, or the water, or in the sky—whatever—let's do it, because frankly, I'm gettin' sick and tired of waitin' to see the big world I mostly just read about all my life in those stacks of picturesque National Geographics I keep, why, I'm not sure, except maybe to keep alive in my own mind the dream of seeing these places; or places I'd seen on the Discovery channel, 'specially where all those wonderful, exotic creatures live that we love to imagine seeing. More than anything else I think I want to see a rhino in the wild. Strange, huh? There's just something about them—so tough and threatening looking, that thick hide and almost ludicrously huge horn, but then, those sad, little drooping eyes that can't see much beyond that horn and that show how vulnerable they really are. And, in truth, there're not many left. So we better get goin' before they're all gone.'"

I put down my notebook and take a deep breath, a breath that seems to come from some place below where I normally breathe from. Then it rises right up to my head, making everything feel suddenly lighter and clearer. This writing feels good, but there's another kind of writing I must do.

I turn to a fresh sheet of paper.

Dear Mother,

First off, please forgive me for not getting in touch. I had to get away for a while, to think about things, because everything in my neatly wound life was coming undone. It's been hard, but I'm beginning to answer some questions I didn't even know how to ask until now.

I don't want to go on about myself because the reason for writing is to do with you, so I'll get right to the point: you must not be afraid to tell Father what YOU want. Don't waste another day. If you want to pursue that career in art history you always thought about but never did, let him know; even if it's something simple like going for a walk and a picnic in Central Park on a May afternoon, you should tell him. You must teach him to listen to what you need, because I don't think he knows how. It's not that he doesn't want you to be happy.

I hope you're well and I'll get in touch again soon. Oh, Happy Thanksgiving! Sorry I won't be spending it with you this year. My best to Father, too.

Love always,

I decide to drive "up Island," as they say around here, to mail the letter (so she doesn't know what town I'm living in), and, while I'm out, get some things I need—a surfboard and a wet suit, a surfcasting rod, and some warm clothes. Also, I'll stop at the animal shelter Oshanta told me about to look for the dog, hopefully a Labrador, I've wanted to get.

As I travel farther away from Montauk, I notice, more than I'd ever noticed before during my summer trips out here with Katherine, how different the landscape becomes. Maybe it's because Montauk is wilder, less inhabited and "civilized" than the other towns on the South Fork, that I notice the difference more now. And then, caught up as we were in our midsummer, traffic-frenzied push toward our eastern or western destination, everything in-between was basically a big blur of asphalt, fumes and cars. But perhaps I notice the difference mostly because, rather than simply enjoying a sojourn here, I feel I live here now, that I'm part of the landscape.

I turn off the highway to Riverhead. The last time I was here a few years ago, it was still fairly quaint. But now I see one big-box shopping center after another. Efficient, I suppose, but efficiency isn't everything. And I wonder what the effect of being inside these boxes has upon how we think? Perhaps there's a new evolving brain: a brain primarily keyed to choosing what to consume amongst myriad rows of goods, most of which we don't actually need and that simply clutter our lives and our world even more.

How lucky I am to be living where I am! I can't wait to get back. I find the post office, mail my letter and turn back east.

I come to Wainscot, where Oshanta said I would find an animal shelter. I spot a sign and hear dogs barking in the distance. My heart starts to beat harder.

I tell the young woman I'm looking for a black Lab, preferably young. She shows me the only one, about two years old. His owners had to move to the city and thought he wouldn't be happy there, she explains. He had been well-cared for and had a happy disposition, though this was becoming less apparent since the days began to stretch into weeks that he'd been at the shelter. This is not the busiest time of year for adopting animals, and most people are looking for younger dogs, she says.

Well, he certainly appears happy as I approach, though perhaps he perks up for all potential saviors who pause by his cage. I stick my hand in to pet his head, which he lifts upward as he closes his eyes and seems to smile, whimpering softly, not despondently as if to say "poor me," but expectantly, hopefully, as in "how 'bout me? I promise I'll be really good, won't ask for too much, and, seriously, I don't chew slippers or bite mailmen." It's a risk, getting a two-year old dog, but I think it's pretty hard to ruin a Lab.

"What's his name?"

"Darth for short," the attendant says. "The boy in the family that owned him was a Star Wars fan, I guess. His full name is Darth Vader."

"I suppose it's too late to change his name. Well, let's hope his name doesn't reflect his personality. You certainly don't look sinister and threatening, do you Darth?"

Darth can hardly contain his exuberance as I lead him out to the car on his rope. He wags his tail so hard the whole back half of his body wags with it, jumps eagerly into the back seat and looks around with obvious relish, as if to say "Boy, I'm glad to be back in one of these." He gives me a big lick on the side of my face.

Leaving Wainscot, I see a surf shop off to the left and pull in. A young blond-headed store clerk helps me pick out a dry suit, a necessity for surfing in the colder water temperatures, and a long board, preferable for beginners, he says.

"Do you know where I might get some lessons?"

"Just about everyone's gone now, north to ski or somewhere south to surf. You picked a strange time to learn, Man—the middle of November, though, in terms of the waves and having fewer surfers to share them with, it's actually a great time."

"Yes, well, it just worked out that way. I've been coming out here for years in the summer, but never got around to it. And now I'm living here and have the time. Maybe I'll just find someone surfing on the beach and ask him."

"Yeah, you could do that. Actually, I plan on staying through Christmas, 'til we close. So I could maybe give you a few. I'll be going out anyway. Where do you live?"

"That's great. In Montauk. When would you be available?"

"Well, we're closed for the next two days."

"Do you have a piece of paper handy? Here's my number and how you get to my house." I draw him a map.

"Man, that's in-between two of the awesomest areas—Turtle Cove and Cavett's Cove. We don't get out there because there's no access, unless you walk real far down the beach, and then you have to get the tide just right so you don't have to walk across all those rocks. Wow, am I psyched!"

"Terrific. My name's Paul, by the way." I shake his hand.

"Mine's Brent."

"See you tomorrow, around noon?"

Coming into Montauk, I see a fishing shop off to the right next to a market. "This is the last stop, I promise, Darth. I'll run in and get some chow for us and a fishing rod and we'll be on our way home." His brown eyes glisten and he barks one short bark, his head nodding as if to say "Yes!"

The Surf

It's almost noon. I start to put on my dry suit. Darth seems to know what one is, for he's getting very excited, running to the door, crying—more like singing, actually. There's a knock at the door.

"Brent, come in. You're right on time."

"Wow, this is a fantastic place. I've seen it from a distance down on the beach and wondered who might live here."

"I've only been here a short time. A musician owns it, and I've rented it for the winter."

"Hey, boy." Brent pets Darth. "You sure seem psyched."

"I think he knows we're going surfing."

Even though I took Darth just once for a short walk down to the beach when we arrived the day before, he knows exactly how to get to the steps, taking charge as our self-appointed guide.

"The waves look clean and they're breaking just right," Brent says pausing to survey the scene at the top of the stairs.

The cold, salty wind nips at my face. "I wonder how cold the water is."

"It's probably around 50 to 55—warmer than the air."

Darth reaches the bottom first, runs directly to the water, waits for a wave to break and plunges in.

"On my trips out to Amagansett in the summers, I did a little body surfing, so I have some sense of how to time a wave."

"Good. Timing is everything, as they say. You have to learn to read the waves, see how they're breaking—the direction, the height, the intervals between them. Once you learn when to take a wave, then all you have to do is ride with its power. Of course, there're first the little skills of learning to balance yourself on the board, to paddle and then stand. They're not easy, but on a long board they're a little easier."

I wade into the water a bit, lie flat on the board, then sit up and try to straddle it, which manages to make me feel singularly uncoordinated.

"Standing is actually easier, if you get the right wave. Okay, I'm going to go out first and you just watch me, to get the image in your mind of how you should stand and how to time the ride. It's always better than explaining. Then after I come in, we'll go out together."

Brent glides effortlessly through the water, his arms stroking cleanly in a perfect rhythm through the glassy surface. Even when he comes upon a looming swell, he rides smoothly over its top without breaking this rhythm, like some kind of sleek, fluid creature that belongs to the sea. Since we came from the sea, maybe this grace in the water is deeply imbedded in a remote corner of our brains, requiring only some dedicated submersion to be stirred from its long sleep.

Brent is straddling his board where the waves begin to form, bobbing with the swells, turned to the south awaiting the right wave. He sees one approaching, probably feels it as much, a swell traveling from a thousand miles away across the Atlantic to climax as a wave upon this beach. He paddles to turn himself around, ready for the ride, looks back and sees it beginning to rise right behind him. He moves his feet on to the board, crouching low to keep his balance; he starts gliding down the face now, propelled in unison with the wave in its unfurling, balanced at that precarious point between losing the wave and being overcome by it.

He rides it forward, then suddenly dips to the side and slightly backwards, playing with this wave, as if in defiance of its power. Yet his form seems small and fragile compared to the wave, poised so vulnerably in its palm. There's a kind of beautiful dance, a balancing act going on: the ocean is being given its due respect by the man who, through his understanding of the wave's dynamics and his finely tuned control over his body and board, is in return granted the grace of the wave.

Brent gets as much out of this wave as he can, riding it to just a few feet from the shoreline. He jumps off, grabs his board and heads toward me. He looks about as happy as a human possibly can, that kind of sheer, unadulterated happiness we often see in children but rarely in adults.

"It was just awesome." It seems he wants to say more, to try to describe it to me in more detail, but he just shakes his head and smiles.

"It was awesome just watching you out there. I think I ought to wait to attempt those little dips in and out of the wave you were doing so deftly, though."

"Oh, the cutbacks. Yeah, I don't mean for you to try to do those yet. I just couldn't help myself, the wave was so fine. Okay, you ready?"

"Sure."

"Now, the most important steps are, number one, when to take the wave, two, how fast you get up on the board, and three, standing in the middle of the board and keeping its nose just out of the water. The more experienced you get, the farther back on the board you can stand—to do those cutbacks I did—or the farther forward—to hang ten and do other kinds of fancy tricks. I'll let you know what wave to take and when. I'm going to swim out with you without my board, so I can help you stay on yours and get you ready for the ride. By the way, don't be surprised if you fall right away, because hardly anyone can stand for long on his first try."

As I start to paddle my way out, fighting the incoming surf, it becomes readily apparent how much strength and stamina the sport demands, considerably more than I currently possess. Not only do I have to fight the waves to the fore, but also to the side as my body constantly tenses and tries to adjust to maintain balance on the board. I tip off and struggle to pull myself back on. My whole body aches from the effort and my breathing is labored. I try to shift my focus, from thinking about how strained and exhausted I feel and how am I possibly going to make it to where the waves begin when we're only halfway there now, to thinking "as if" I were a sleek creature who belongs to the sea.

Brent, swimming smoothly beside me, signals that this is where we'll wait for a wave. It's strangely calm here; a welcome respite between the struggle to arrive and the much more challenging struggle to come of making my way in. I ask Brent if he wants to hold on to my board, but he doesn't seem winded in the least and shakes his head no. Our gazes fixed to the endless expanse beyond, we search for that one swell amidst the glassy rolling surface. The rhythmic rocking motion eases some of the tension from my body. I begin to relax, yet at the same time all my senses, from my toes to the top of my brain, seem extraordinarily alert. I scan the horizon from east to west, sea and sky merging to create a vast blue sphere in which I float. I feel a humbling sense of smallness, but not insignificance, rather an aliveness of *being*. I close my eyes and try to imagine for a moment that this might be what it is like at the very beginning of life, rocked back and forth, safely floating in a sea of boundless love.

"Paul, Paul, get ready! It's coming!" I open my eyes. A big swell is only about 35 feet out. Brent helps me turn my board around.

"Okay, now, quick, get your feet on the board. There you go!" I feel the sea rising beneath me, lifting me up, thrusting me forward with a sudden surge of exhilarating speed. I'm teetering back and forth. I'm going to fall and crash. No, stay calm, center yourself. God, I'm actually riding this wave! I lean a bit too much to the left. Down into the heart of the wave I go, a wall of water rising behind me then falling just ahead of me. I know how lucky I am to be here rather than a foot forward or back. I see my board go off to the right, but caught in the whirl of the wave, it could possibly be sent sailing back toward me.

I take a big breath and dive deep underwater, heading for shore. I remember as a boy how I challenged myself to swim as far as I could underwater. I loved this world under the sea.

I've gone as far as I can go, my lungs now beginning to hurt. I head for the surface, knowing I'm not far from the shore, as the sun's light is close above and the sandy bottom near below. Coming up, I scan the surface and off to the west see a figure on a board, paddling in to shore. He looks toward me and waves. Darth, spotting a piece of me after probably much fretful gazing and pacing the shoreline, plunges joyfully into the water to meet me.

"Man, I was worried about you for a while," Brent says as we walk to the beach.

"Darth was too. You just disappeared."

"I was nervous about getting hit by the board, so I swam underwater as far as I could."

"Which was amazingly far. So, what did you think?"

"Well, I didn't stay on for long, but I felt as if I was beginning to get a sense of it, the fundamentals of it, and I wasn't really afraid at any point."

"Yeah, you looked pretty good for your first time out. The first time out is the key. People either get overwhelmed or hooked."

"I know I have to get in better shape, because by the time I stood on the board, I was so winded from getting out there, I didn't have enough to sustain a decent ride even if I had the ability. Maybe it will help if I start running."

"You know what would be better—there's a spa, Gurney's, down the road from here that has an indoor saltwater swimming pool. That's what you should do to condition yourself. Laps in the pool."

"Okay. Great."

"So, you're hooked? You want to go out again after you rest some?"

My body feels as wrung-out weary as it ever has, but also deeply satisfied from probably the greatest challenge it's ever had; then the great rush, the thrill, and that feeling of ... I smile and nod my head yes.

Thanksgiving

Journal entry, November 24:
Sometimes I feel as if I'm floating through space. Unconnected to anything, I'm seized by a vertiginous terror, a terror I paradoxically experience as an exhilarating rush. It's much like the feeling of being thrust forward on the face of a wave, not knowing where I'm going or by what forces I happen to be doing what I am—virtually walking on water, defying all logic and known boundaries. Falling into this void beyond the known boundaries of who I am, I'm feeling my way to defining myself in a different way.

How much I've let myself be defined by forces outside of me—by my father, my colleagues and superiors at work, by some image I had of what I was supposed to be—I never realized before. Only when the wave came crashing down, washing everything away, leaving me with the silence that comes when there's nothing left but you looking at yourself rather than a reflection of you, could I begin to realize.

It's really quite incredible, this frenzied whirl of energy, all to feed an insatiable need for something as fleeting as admiration. Yet, one doesn't create himself as if in a solitary laboratory. So, if the key is to learn to steer from within, which is achieved by building a sense of self from within, how does one do this when there is no self to begin with?

I put down my pen and look out the window at the now churning sea from a northeast wind that had been intensifying since early morning. I think back on my surfing of the day before, on that ineffable something about the experience neither Brent nor I could articulate. I pick up my pen again.

Maybe the mystery and thrill lie in that critical and delicate equilibrium between the wave's power and your own, an equilibrium that can't be achieved without first gaining a degree of control over yourself. And this can only be accomplished by disciplined developing of strength and technique that requires, in turn, constant submersion into the humbling sea where you will be tossed about—without a care in the world for your fate—through the walls and valleys of many trials and errors. But perhaps the real key is in knowing there's always the possibility of another wave confronting you with something you've never experienced before.

It's Thanksgiving, the first one I've ever awakened to alone. Well, not completely alone, Darth reminds me, as he greets me with a generous lick on the face and an energetic wag of his tail.

"Hey, boy. I'm sure glad I've got you." The phone rings.

"Madeline, good to hear from you, and Happy Thanksgiving to you too ... I'm doing fine. Got myself a great dog, reminds me of the Lab I had as a child ... Yes, I wrote to my parents, but I don't want them to know my address or phone number, not yet anyway ... Oh, I'm going to spend it with some very nice people I met ... I don't know when. I'm not really thinking about it at all. Maybe never, though that's unrealistic. I certainly don't have an unlimited savings to live on; enough for a while longer, at any rate. I took my first surfing lesson. It was thrilling. I'm learning a lot of things. I'm glad you called, and I do miss you. Take care."

It seems as if I was talking to someone in a far-away world, though it was the world that felt distant, not Madeline, whose voice was as close and warm as it always had been. Strange, how I miss her more than anyone else. It's the unspoken bond between us, the trust I have that comes from a sense she's one of those rare people who sees underneath the outside trappings, for whom there's never the need to impress, and who appreciates that quiet voice inside.

Thinking about Thanksgiving, it occurs to me I should bring an offering of some kind to supper this afternoon. "I know, Darth—let's go try to catch a fish with my new rod."

The wind, only partly blocked by the bluffs, is still blowing hard, spitting bits of sand. Darth doesn't seem to be bothered, but I don't know how long I'll withstand it. Yet just the possibility of catching a striped bass, which are running now according to the man in the store where I bought my rod, makes any hardships of the effort worthwhile. An incredibly delicious fish, one of my favorite when we came out for the summers, striped bass had been unavailable for a few years, illegal to catch due to over-fished stocks. Like the prized bay scallops from this area's waters, striped bass had virtually disappeared, apparently only this year making a comeback. I tighten the hood on my jacket and head toward the shore.

Not far to the east I see a man casting into the surf from his perch on a rock a ways out. As the waves roll in, the rock and the man from the waist down are engulfed in dark grayish-green water and salt spray glistening white in the rising sun. To my amazement, he doesn't appear to waver at all, as if he were attached somehow to the rock, his green waders blending with the sea and his hair and beard blowing in the wind. A black Lab frolics along the shore; he and Darth spot each other, run to meet and take off together cavorting on the edge of the sea.

Although it's been a long time since I've handled a fishing rod, my hands seem to have kept a memory of the skill. But the wind is posing an extra challenge, as I cast and the line is blown back to almost where I stand. I try a heavier plug and then a cast with less air, just skimming the surface. Now there's the challenge of my hands trying to feel when I have a bite in the midst of such a turbulent sea; given the length of time since I've fished, normal conditions would be enough to contend with.

Looking down to the east, I see the fisherman walking toward me. The dogs are trotting alongside, curiously sniffing the contents of a bag slung over his shoulder.

"It's a tough one out here today, but I got me one. What a fight he gave! Must be about a ten-pounder."

He opens the bag and shows me the huge fish. I had never seen a whole striped bass before, never realized how big they are. With wide black stripes over a silvery body still wet and gleaming, its eyes and mouth opened wide as if in a permanently startled state, the fish appeared as if its life was only momentarily suspended, awaiting its return to the sea.

"What kind a lure ya' usin'?"

"Oh, a plug. The fellow at the fishing tackle store in town highly recommended it." Because the man speaks with a strong accent, like a southern drawl mixed with an English accent, it's difficult to understand readily what he's saying. His speech sounds like what Oshanta described to me as that of a Bonacker, local folk who descend from the Puritans from northern England who settled around Accabonac Harbor in East Hampton in the mid-1600s, becoming farmers and fishermen.

"Well, Henry woulda' told ya right. Pretty nasty day though, usually find only us die-hard Bonackers out here. Should have yourself some waders, get out there closer to the action."

"Does that help?"

"Helps ya to feel more where the fish is, where it's moving to, and when it's hooked. Like the old days when we haulseined, when we were right in there with the fish. That was real fishin'."

"What's haulseining"?

"A kind of ocean fishing we did with nets, mostly for stripers when they were running. We'd launch a dory out from the beach, against the breakin' waves, row her out to where the fish were running and set the net. The net'd be hooked up on shore to two truck winches, one at either end, and when the net was filled with fish, we'd pull her in with the winch and us half in and out of the water, tying her up to keep the fish in and haulin' her to shore, fightin' the waves breakin' on us and the fish fightin' to get free. Timing had to be just right—the launch, the haulin'—and everything was happening faster than you could think it. Can still feel it through to my bones—the thrill of beatin' the breakers and gettin' the dory out beyond 'em, the net cuttin' through my hands in the icy water and us haulin' at once, like we was a kind a net too, all tied together. But I can't really 'xplain. Those kind a 'speriences just too darn big to squeeze into some little words.

"Anyway, the D.E.C. put an end to it, banned haulseining sayin' it was dirty fishin', that it killed other fish we'd throw out. What a joke. Look at these draggers with their miles of nets and these longliners with thousands of hooks that hook anything and everything. Now that's dirty fishin', and on a huge scale. We're just about 50 baymen out here on the East End, and haulseining was the way our families fished for 250 years. Striped bass was our biggest catch. It wasn't us that overfished 'em either. It was the big commercial fishing boats and the sport fishermen. But the government punished us more than anyone, just took away our way of life."

Listening intently, I suddenly feel a hard drag on my line, and, caught off guard, almost lose my balance.

"Hold on tight, now fella, and reel 'em in. You got 'em."

The fish is fighting so hard, I almost don't want to catch it. But I do want to bring a gift for Thanksgiving, and catching it is certainly better than buying it in the market. I reel in the line determinedly.

Finally, I pull it up on shore.

"Got yourself a nice fish there. Well, enjoy your Thanksgiving, and good day to ya."

"To you, too. Maybe I'll see you again out here. My name is Paul, by the way, and this is Darth. I'm living up there on the bluff for the winter."

"My name is Capem' Harold Lester, and this here's Bubbie. Well, good luck. Hope the wind doesn't get to ya. Ya know what they say about Montauk: stay here long enough and the wind'll drive ya crazy. Me and Bubbie is proof enough." He throws his head back, his beard and reddish but graying hair blowing in the wind, and lets out a hearty laugh as he and his dog disappear in the morning mist.

It's time to go to Oshanta's great aunt's house. I take the fish out of the broiler and do a taste-test: it's done just right. The one thing I know I can cook well is fish. Darth looks at me, obviously wanting to know if he's to be included in the eating of this wonderfully smelling dish. I hadn't planned to include him, but it didn't seem right to leave him on Thanksgiving.

When I arrive at Olivia Pharaoh's, I knock on the door in hopes Oshanta will answer.

"Paul, I'm so glad you decided to come." She kisses me lightly on the cheek. "I just got back from my trip to Albany and New York City this morning."

"Did you make any progress?"

"Yes, some. We'll talk about it later."

"I caught a fish this morning and thought I'd contribute it to dinner."

"How thoughtful. Bertrand brought clams but we don't have any fish."

"Oh, do you think it would be okay to bring my dog in? I hated to leave him alone."

"Of course."

"I got him at the animal shelter you told me about. His name is Darth."

"Hey, Darth." I'm impressed with his manners. He sits and offers his paw to Oshanta.

The living room is filled with about 20 people of many sizes, ages and hues, from as white as me to charcoal black. A long table in the middle is laden with food, including a large turkey, cranberry jelly, relish and bread, clam pie, pumpkin pie and something called samp Oshanta tells me is a Montauk specialty made from boiled corn. Oshanta finds a place for the striped bass, then brings me to where her great aunt is sitting.

"Happy Thanksgiving, and thank you for having me, Olivia."

"Mr. Collins, so nice to see you." She has the same warm and wise smile she had when I first met her. Next to her stood a tall, beige-skinned man of about my age, dressed in a dark suit with a minister's black and white collar. "This is my great nephew, Samson Fowler Occum."

His ebony eyes appear to read everything they see in the bat of an eyelash; his high forehead and erect posture convey a dignity that approaches aloofness. But then, this latter impression might arise from my own misperception: that outside the walls of a church, ministers always seem uncomfortable, as if the chasm between their high ideals and the base realities of the world is impossible for them to bridge.

"His great great grandfather was Samson Occum, a Mohegan from Connecticut who came to Montauk as a teacher and minister in the mid-1700s and then married Mary Fowler, a Montaukett. He knew English, Greek, Latin, philosophy and theology, and because of him, the Montauketts were said to be the most educated of all the tribes. He created the first wooden alphabet blocks, wrote hymns to Native American melodies that are still sung in Presbyterian churches, and went to England to try to get funds to start what was supposed to be the first college for Indians, Dartmouth College. Samson is following in his forefather's footsteps as a great powwaw, our word for priest or holy man: Yale Divinity School, minister in the most popular church around, the Congregational Church in Sag Harbor. And he'll help build the school for Indians from all the tribes of Long Island on our ancestral lands, Indian Fields.

"Then we'll build a museum, with the guidance of my grandson Bertrand, a museum which will gather in one place all of our proud history and memories now scattered far and wide. Thus we'll become a proud leader of the Paumonok tribes once again."

"Well, Aunt Olivia, I'd like to start a school," Samson says slowly, respectfully, "one that would combine the best of a western classical education with the culture and beliefs of Native Americans, but I don't think I'd want it to be exclusively for Native Americans. White people need to learn about our culture as much as we need to learn about theirs. We're accepted into their schools, after all. We've made some progress since the eighteenth century, Aunt Olivia." He smiles and pats her on the shoulder.

Not to be easily placated, Olivia responds in a firm voice. "Remember what happened to your great great grandfather: after all his hard work over two-and-a-half years raising money in England for a school, he was betrayed by his white colleague Wheelock who changed his mind and decided instead of an Indian school, it should be for whites too, and instead of in Connecticut, it should be far away in New Hampshire, where there were no Montauketts or Mohegans. So, though Occum's money actually founded Dartmouth, it was not an Indian school and Occum never taught there.

"As far as making progress, that may be true, but in many ways, I don't think we have. In some places, I think it's even worse, with the alcohol problems and no sense of belonging to either white or Indian culture and no sense of dignity or hope on those sad reservations. I've even heard that children, just children mind you, are killing themselves on these reservations in South Dakota. Look at us here, still trying to get our rightful land back after 300 years of trying, and white men drilling holes in it."

"When we're all gathered around the table, I'll tell everyone what I found out in Albany, and what everyone can do to help," Oshanta says. "This is a perfect opportunity, for rarely are so many of us together as we are today, even with some relations from other parts of Long Island."

"Yes, I think it's time," Olivia says. "Here's Bertrand. Bertrand, would you call everyone to the table. Oh, do you know Mr. Collins?"

"Yes, Oshanta introduced us. A pleasure to see you." He looks as dazzlingly handsome as the first time I saw him emerging from the water, though he appears more serious, his eyes and mouth unsmiling. He's carrying a small drum decorated with feathers and colorful paintings of birds, deer and fish.

"What a beautiful drum."

"Thank you. I made it a number of years ago. I play it a little almost every day." He turns it around in his hands. "A drum was used by my people to call the elders of the tribe together for important meetings or rituals. It is said to be the most universal instrument, I think because its sound resembles that of nature and of life—the beating of a heart, the sea pounding against the sand, of thunder in the sky—and also for the simple reason that its shape is a circle." He looks me squarely in the eyes. "As you probably know, the circle was the most significant shape in most cultures, at least until Christianity came along with its symbol of the cross and its division between things of the world and the spirit, between me and you."

"Now, now Bertrand, I beg to differ," Samson interjects in a scholarly tone. "Actually, if you look at some of the ancient Christian texts, such as the Winchester Bible of the early twelfth century, you'll see many circular symbols. The Wheel of Fortune is an image found often in medieval Christian texts, as is the Tree of Life and Death with the figures of Adam and Eve beneath its crown and a snake twirled around the trunk symbolizing the circle of life and death. The original messages of Christ—'Love thy neighbor as thyself,' 'Judge not that you may not be judged,' 'I and the Father are one,'—are not ones of division but unity, my dear Bertrand.

"And this is the same message—that God is in us and in everything, and that through good works and right living we can become more like him—we see in Buddhism and Hinduism in the circular symbol of the mandala. We see it in Black Elk's mystical vision of the 'hoop of the nation, all the nations' hoops ... and I saw myself in the central mountain of the world ... But the central mountain is everywhere,' and in the eloquent words of Chief Seattle, 'One thing we know, there is only one God. No man, be he Red Man or White Man, can be apart. We are brothers after all.'"

"You paint as rosy and pretty a picture as your church's stained glass window, Samson," Bertrand says with much gravity as he looks down at his drum and moves his hand slowly around its rim. "But you are leaving out the dark side of this picture: that the church's corruption of Christ's message—one ruled by judgment and division rather than unity and love—is the one that dominated. And that in Black Elk's vision, he saw the end of his nation, the Sioux, and of all the great Native American nations which would be destroyed by white men. And that Chief Seattle's words, a passionate plea to the white man to protect and honor the land his tribe was being forced to sell, fell on deaf ears. So much for unity."

Although Bertrand doesn't seem to be directing his words toward me, I can't help but feel uneasy. A sense of deep-seated guilt, a piece of that great national guilt over the crimes committed against Native Americans that's kept buried because it's too shameful for us to confront honestly, wells up in me. I look anxiously about me.

Sensing this, Oshanta taps my arm and says spiritedly, "But Thanksgiving is a day of unity, so Bertrand, shall we call everyone together now?"

Bertrand begins beating the drum and chanting in a low three-note melody, *"Wequo-sew, Manito, Taw-but-nee, Manito."* Everyone stops talking and gathers around the table. Olivia sits at one end and Samson at the other.

"Thank you, Bertrand. Now that we have greeted and thanked the Great Spirit in song, Samson will say the blessing," Olivia says. In a deep, resonant voice, so melodious it sounds almost as if he's singing, he begins:

> *We thank the Great Spirit,*
> *for this bountiful harvest,*
> *for the good fortune that gathers us from far and wide to*
> *share and give thanks for what we have and for all the*
> *Great Spirit's creations that on this beautiful Earth abide.*

*To the sky that brings the sun and the rain that grow the
seeds of our trees and grain.
To the winds of the north, south, east and west,
To all creatures of the sea, plants and beasts,
To our ancestors who from beyond to us speak,
Even to those who in anger we'd call enemy,
Let us seek understanding and harmony by remembering
to give thanks and to pray that all our thoughts and deeds
reflect those of the Great Spirit's every day.*

"That was beautiful, Samson. Now, before we enjoy this great feast, I have a few words to say and then Runs with the Wind will speak. I thank you all for coming here today for this gathering of great historic importance. It is fitting that it's the day of our fall harvest festival, the day most celebrated by our forefathers, because it also marks a time of renewed hope and pride in the long history of our tribe. This is the first of more gatherings to come, as Runs with the Wind will explain, and it is a good time for me to pass on to the youth the staff of leadership, in the form of this walking stick that belonged to the great Stephen Talkhouse Pharaoh who, as you all know, was famous for how far and fast he could walk. I give it as a symbol of how far we will go from here, in securing our land where we all can live again, in building a school for our children and becoming a proud people again. Not to live in the past, but to be proud of our past and carry forth the dignity, the seeking of truth, respect for life and love of beauty that our people hold so dear.

"My son Nathan would be the one to receive this staff if he had lived, and my brother's son, Runs with the Wind's father, if he had lived, or his wife, Cornelia, if she were healthier in mind and body. So, to the next generation it will go. Though this has never been done before, I present it in honor of not one person but of three: first to my grandson, Bertrand, who will keep it in trust and teach a respect and love for the beauty and skills of our artistic traditions; to Samson Occum, my great nephew who will build our school and teach the truth of our great traditions; and to Runs with the Wind, my great niece, who will do the important work of securing our land. If there is anyone who disagrees, please speak your mind now."

"Thank you, grandmother. This is a great honor you bestow upon me, and I hope I can live up to your wishes. But I think that the staff should be given to Runs with the Wind, for she will be doing most of the work until we have our land, then perhaps she can pass it to Samson and then he can to me."

"Yes, that makes very good sense to me," Samson concurred.

"So it shall be. Runs with the Wind, it is with great faith that I offer this staff to you."

Oshanta strokes and turns around in her hands the dark, gnarled, cherry wood staff, nicked and grooved from age and the many miles it has traveled.

"Thank you, Great Aunt Olivia. And thanks to Bertrand, Samson and all of you for your confidence in me. I hope I will bring honor to you, to my mother, whom I visited yesterday and who sends her best to everyone, to the memory of my father, to my ancestor Stephen Talkhouse Pharaoh whose dignity and accomplishments in mind and body brought great honor to our tribe, and to all my ancestors. It will be a hard journey, to get our land back, but I have taken the first steps, and now you must help me. I want you all to gather whatever you can—letters, notes, clothing, photographs—of your family history, as far back as you can to the present, for we need to create a historical record, one as continuous as possible. We have to prove to the government that, contrary to popular belief, we have always been and are today a true tribe. We have to show records of birth certificates and genealogies. I have gotten copies of most of the public historical records, from the Town library and historical society, and from the State Museum in Albany, but most of the material, particularly written along with some artifacts, remains with us. There are many more artifacts in The American Museum of Natural History in New York and at the Smithsonian Museum in Washington, which I plan to document, and some I hope to obtain.

"And of course we have the books by the historian John Strong and archaeologist Gaynell Stone which are invaluable studies of the excavations at Indian Fields and other sites and of Montauk history and culture.

"In any gatherings you may have from now on, please take notes or record them on a tape recorder, as you see I'm doing. Elders should try to record their memories of times past on tape, too. I have a video camera that I will lend to anyone who would like to borrow it for this purpose. I hope to have regular meetings like this, perhaps once a month, so that we can keep in contact. I just came back from Albany to speak to our state legislators, who at least gave me letters of support for our efforts and said they would do everything they can to protect Indian Fields until we can get our federal status as a tribe and prove our claim to our historic lands stolen from us through devious treaties and deeds. The way our claim was denied in 1909 by Judge Blackmar in New York State Supreme Court was to say we didn't exist as a tribe. With such a ruling, we were not even entitled to a reservation, as the Shinnecocks in Southampton at least have, and indeed, most recognized tribes have. This injustice we're going to right.

"So, to the strength and future of the Montauks, thank you, and let us now enjoy this bountiful feast."

Painting These Waters to Life

"Thank you for inviting me, Oshanta. It was a wonderful dinner. I enjoyed meeting your relatives and friends, and hope no one objected to my presence."

"I'm sure no one did. Why would anyone?"

"Well, I felt a little resentment from Bertrand, but maybe I imagined it."

"Oh, sometimes Bertrand gets into his angry-at-everything-about-white men mode, but it's nothing personal. As a matter of fact, he wants us to come visit his studio now. Bertrand has been through a lot. As I mentioned before, his parents buried their Native American identity. So, as he became more interested in his heritage upon leaving home for college, he grew further apart from them. He hadn't communicated with them for a while. Then, on New Year's Eve in Wisconsin seven years ago, they were killed in a car accident by a drunk driver. He partly blames himself, for not having accepted them on their own terms, but then their death also seemed to confirm in him his notion that whether we join white culture or not, we're equally its victims. Since his loss, and then my father dying and my mother becoming ill, Bertrand and I have gotten very close."

"What happened to your father, if you don't mind me asking?"

"My father was an intelligent man, too smart for the laborer's work he did which, I think, caused him to ruin himself with alcohol.

Unlike Bertrand, he lacked the guidance from his parents to push himself to achieve. When he died, my mother, who was very sensitive to begin with, had a severe breakdown. She's in a good hospital in New York City where I visit her often when I'm there. Even if I had the time to take care of her, she's just too ill to live outside of a hospital environment: about half of her waking time she's normal, and the other half, she'll sit on the floor for hours, rocking back and forth, saying she's on a ship lost at sea, bound in shackles in the dark. Her great grandfather on her father's side had come from Africa, and he must have told her terrible stories when she was young. Doctors have tried everything—from various medications to pretending to unlock her chains and set her free."

Words of sympathy seem pathetically paltry, but I must say something. "I'm so sorry. It's one of the saddest stories I think I've ever heard."

We walk out from the porch into the early evening. "Yes, it's very sad." She looks toward the water ahead. "I think at times we all feel we're lost at sea."

I stop in my tracks, her words hitting me hard—the feeling of being lost at sea since coming out here. Then, after a few moments, turning her gaze to the sky, the stars just beginning to brighten, she adds in a spirited tone, "But then, I'll look at the sky and instead feel I'm on an exciting journey as limitless as my mind wants it to be. And speaking of going on an exciting journey," her voice rising with keen anticipation as she points in the near distance, "Bertrand's studio is right over there."

The air is brisk and smells of cedar, pine and the sea, exciting Darth who, having been very patient and well-behaved during dinner, now figures his just reward is to go for a long romp and perhaps even a quick swim. I call him back.

Oshanta knocks on the door. "Welcome!" Bertrand greets us in an expansive mood, quite different from a little while before. "To man, woman and beast, and within these weird walls, I hope to delight, or not to offend at least."

Oshanta laughs. "Thanks for giving us fair warning."

The cabin is almost identical to Olivia's. We enter a small kitchen, then a large beamed living room with a stone fireplace on one side, a room off to the side, which appears to be a bedroom, and another small room. Instead of two windows facing east to the water as in Olivia's house, Bertrand has made the entire wall into a window. More light comes from oversized skylights; I look up and see trees and the stars beyond. In front of the fireplace are two leather chairs on either side of a sofa and a glass-topped coffee table. A large Navaho-looking rug covers much of the floor. The rest of the space is taken up with various paintings propped up on easels and others leaning against the two remaining wood walls. Illumination comes from track lighting along the beams and two six-foot tall iron candelabras on either side of the hearth where a fire blazes.

"What a great place," I say looking across the harbor, slivers of moonlight swimming over the surface like silvery fish.

"Thank you. The big windows make it a bit drafty in the winter when the wind whips across from the northeast. But on the plus side, I get a lot of solar heat when the sun's out."

"Can we just wander around and look at your paintings?" Oshanta asks.

"Be my guest. The one on the easel over there and the one next to it are two I've just finished, so they're still wet."

We walk closer to one. It's about two-and-a-half feet square; the material used for the painting seems to be a very light colored hide of some kind, showing the creases and slight discolorations of an animal skin. The colors have a muted, almost antique look to them. The image of a coiled snake takes up the central part of the picture. In the center of it is a man wielding a sword about to strike at the head of the snake, whose mouth is wide open, seemingly about to bite the man. In each of the four corners of the painting is the face of a Native American, imbedded in the background of the earth in one corner, the sky in another, the sea in the third and a forest in the fourth. Each of the figures has the slightly sad but proud expression found in many historical photographs of Native Americans.

"Every time I see your work again, it has changed. I remember when your painting reminded me of Kandinsky's."

"Ah, yes. That was a very long time ago, or at least so it seems. I didn't have any focus then, any personal way of seeing things. Images would just float by and I'd use them. Now they don't come from out there as much as from in here." He taps a point in the middle of his chest.

"Yes, I can see that. There's also something different about the paint, and you're not using canvas."

"I'm mixing my own paints now, from natural pigments. Many of them I find right around here. I can make a spectrum of reds, from a brilliant reddish-orange to a deep scarlet, from the sumac bush. For dark blues to purples, I use pokeweed, chokecherry and elderberry. I create browns from oak bark and black from its galls, greens from nettle, and yellows from elderberry leaves and goldenrod. Olivia taught me all of it. The colors are so much more alive than oils from a tube. As far as canvas, I was starting to feel uninspired by it, then I tried linen, which was more interesting but too delicate. About a year ago I went to the new Museum of the American Indian downtown, and saw a wonderful Pueblo Indian painting on buffalo hide. It was a perfect off-white with grayish discolorations here and there. So, to try to duplicate it I buy thin pieces of leather and bleach them in the sun. It's pretty close. I don't like stretching it onto a wood frame, though. I would rather just hang it with the jagged edges of a natural skin. But that would be too difficult to mount for a gallery show."

"I recognize the figures of Samson Occum and Stephen Pharaoh, those high cheek bones, copper skin and black, shoulder-length hair. And I believe that is Queen Maria, my favorite image of her, her chin held high, her eyes and mouth set firm and straight, the single white feather in the beaded headband. But I don't know who the fourth is."

"That's Nathan Cuffee, the blind author of *Lords of the Soil*, one of the only two writers I know of from our tribe, the other being Olivia Ward Bush Banks. Here Nathan Cuffee represents the artistic talents of our people, Stephen Pharaoh represents the physical greatness, Samson Occum the intellectual and spiritual abilities, and Queen Maria the indomitable pride in our tribe's heritage, which she showed by fighting for our rights in Washington, and by writing an autobiography."

"Yes. Along with Samson Occum's diary and Olivia Banks' writings, her autobiography is going to be one of the most important documents for me to continue her fight. Unfortunately, only two pages of Banks' play *Indian Trails*, about the Montauks loss of their land, survive. Cuffee not only was the first Montaukett to become a writer, but he was the first Native American from all of Long Island to become one, as far as we know. What a sensitive and handsome face he had.

"It's a brilliant and beautiful painting, Bertrand. Tell me though, who wins? Does the white man cut off the head of the snake, which I assume represents our people and our culture, or does the snake kill the man?"

"The point of having the four figures in the four corners outside of the circle of the snake is that, no matter who wins the fight, fought on the physical, that is the political and social plane, the spiritual values of our people will live on."

I am stunned by the painting. So well painted, and so powerful in its meaning.

"Bertrand, I like this painting so much. Would you sell it to me?"

"Well, thank you, Paul. After the show next month we can talk about it, if you still want it. I haven't thought of a price yet. Do you buy much art?"

"No. And the paintings I have bought are quite different in style. My biggest purchase was a Thomas Cole at a Sotheby auction of Hudson River School artists—it was quite an expenditure but it was one of the few paintings I truly ever loved. But, the spirit of that art doesn't seem too dissimilar to the spirit of this: how people are depicted as an integral part of the landscape around them. I think those nineteenth century painters were trying to capture something of the beautiful new world colonists found upon coming here, before it was gone. You are saying in this painting your outer world may be in danger of disappearing but not the inner world."

Bertrand looks at me with much more curiosity than he had before.

The next painting is about the size of the first but round in shape. The nude figure of a copper-skinned woman with long black hair, her arms outstretched to form the shape of a cross, is descending from a blue sky into a blue-green expanse of water. Arising from the water is a large turtle, upon which there are trees and animals—deer, bears and wolves. Outside the grove of trees are Bosch-like creatures, part man and part animal. Inside of the sun high in the sky are three people, a white man, a brown woman in the middle, and a black man, their arms outstretched, touching their fingertips with each other.

"I recognize part of it as the Algonquian creation myth of the earth being created on the back of a turtle. But I'm not sure of the female figure or the half-man half-animal creatures," Oshanta says.

"It's a painting that combines both Iroquois and Algonquian creation myths. According to Iroquois legend, Sky Woman descends from the heavens to the sea where the earth rose up beneath her and she then created all of its forms from her body. She first increased the land, then created the trees, then the deer, bears and lastly the wolves. Man was created from each of the three animals, so that it was said men's natures were timid, gentle, innocent like a deer; brave, strong, protective like a bear; or aggressive, tribal and bellicose like a wolf. Rather insightful view of humankind, I'd say."

"What about the three human figures in the sun?"

"To tell you the truth, I'm not sure exactly what I intended. But I think they represent both what we were when we were no more than just an idea in the Great Spirit's mind—pure and beautiful—and what we can be, with the ability to return to a state of love and forgiveness, represented by Sky Woman with her outstretched hands, who is not only descending but ascending."

"A note of optimism from the incorrigible skeptic! Bertrand, I'm absolutely in awe. This is a fabulous painting. I like it even more than the other," Oshanta says. The painting is affecting me almost more than I can put into words.

"So do I." After a few moments, I continue. "I think it's mostly to do with the power of the sea, from where everything, even the earth, emerges. Lately, I've been thinking a lot about this power as I watch and listen to the ocean in front of my house. But there's something else here I can't quite put my finger on, something about the people in the sun. Yes! Now I recall. The night I came out here, I found myself standing on a bluff overlooking the ocean, feeling as wild as the sea was that night. I saw dark scenes of my recent life, then nostalgic scenes from my childhood. Suddenly I had a vision: I saw myself as a boy, shining like a star, inside a dark body; and I saw that boy grow larger, until he spread out to the dark periphery of the man, transforming it into a yellow shimmering line, like the sun."

As if to illustrate the image, my hands spread out in front of me and my fingers flutter ever so slightly. Both Bertrand and Oshanta are looking at me wide-eyed. From a nearby table he pours wine into three glasses and, as we raise them to each other, Bertrand says "To what we can be."

Flames of Desire and Fear

It's past midnight. My body wants to sleep, but my mind, stimulated by Bertrand's visual magic, keeps reeling through the myriad colorful scenes of the day: Captain Lester fishing on the rocks; Bertrand playing the painted drum; the face and voice of Samson Fowler Occum; the images of Stephen Pharaoh, Sky Woman, the sea and three people touching hands in the sun. I finally doze off.

Bertrand, Oshanta and I are walking through the woods. We come to a high plateau, where we sit in a circle. Bertrand plays his drum, Oshanta plays a wooden flute and I, the trumpet. A snake arises out of the earth in our midst, so large it spirals high above us. It seems entranced by our music. Then we hear a howling sound, and think it's the wind. Suddenly a huge fire-breathing figure with the head of a coyote and the body of a man appears. He breathes fire upon the snake; it withers and dies. He tries to burn us, but we escape by rising above the flames, to the clouds above the trees. We watch helplessly in horror and sadness as the woods below burns to the ground.

I awake with a start. The dream vanishes, except for the image of a coiled snake and the distant sound of a flute. Unable to retrieve other fragments of the dream or to fall asleep again, I pick up the book closest to me, *Being and Time*. Not exactly bedtime reading, but perhaps its turgid style will prove the perfect sedative.

Yet in-between the semantically difficult and abstruse lines I find some remarkably lucid ones: "The wood in the forest is timber, the mountain a quarry of rock; the river is water-power, the wind is wind in the sails ... Nature can be discovered and defined simply by its presence-at-hand. But when this happens, the Nature which stirs and thrives remains hidden." He goes on to say that seeing Nature as a "thing of use," the Cartesian way of thinking, separates "the real from the ideal" and excludes its "phenomenological," metaphysical and transcendent qualities ... "which, in principle, is still the usual one today."

Interesting—I had never gotten this ecological message when I'd read Heidegger 20 years ago. Unlike with Nietzsche, I'm finding more of an affinity to this philosopher now. He's speaking of an "authentic" way of being to be found in a "primordial," "ecstatical" experience of the phenomena of the world, of Nature, which is all endowed with "spirit," and that this "truth" is covered and uncovering it is the endless process of our becoming. The increasing "coveredness" of the truth and the difficulty in our experiencing an authentic way of Being is primarily the result of the industrialization and mechanization of society and its consequent dulling effect upon the individual's sensibilities.

As to Being's relation to Time: "The irresoluteness of inauthentic existence temporalizes itself in the mode of a making-present which does not await but forgets ... Busily losing himself in the object of his concern, he loses his time in it too. Hence his characteristic way of talking 'I have no time.' But just as he who exists inauthentically is constantly losing time and never has any, the temporality of authentic existence remains distinctive in that such existence, in its resoluteness, never loses time ... for it has, with relation to the present, the *character of a moment of vision."*

After 480 pages of very dense, complex exposition, the philosopher characterizes his treatise as merely a "point of departure" for further investigation into the nature of Being, and also as only "one way we may take" in this investigation, an admirable show of humility not a general feature in the western philosophical tradition: "Our comments ... have shown that what is essential does not lie in its *actuality* as a philosophical 'movement'. Higher than actuality stands *possibility.*" And, like a true, "authentic" philosopher, and, again, more in the style of eastern philosophy, he ends with more questions than possible answers: "Is there a way that leads from primordial time to the meaning of Being? Does time itself manifest itself as the horizon of Being?"

"Horizon of Being"—what fitting words with which to conclude. They echo in my mind, reminding me of ... I close my eyes and see three figures inside a glowing orange-yellow sun. Then I see myself walking through a shad forest, as I had a week ago when I experienced a moment in which I began to understand the meaning of *feeding the fire inside*—to open oneself up to not knowing, to possibility, to the horizon of being.

I awake to Darth barking. Someone is knocking at the door. I look at the clock. It's noon and the sun is shining brightly. It must be Oshanta and Bertrand, here for the walk we had agreed last night we would to take to the Montauk Indian village today if the weather permitted. I throw on my robe.

"Come in. Please excuse me. I'm afraid I stayed up very late reading and overslept. I'll get dressed quickly."

"Must have been a good book," Oshanta says.

"Actually, I thought it would help me fall asleep, because it's an ultra-heavy tome, Heidegger's *Being and Time*, another philosopher I'm re-reading. But instead, I really got into it."

"Now there's one we can agree on—probably my next favorite after Russell and Spinoza," Bertrand exclaims buoyantly. "Reading Heidegger is like listening to jazz for the first time: you have to get used to the complicated language, then after a while you begin to hear the beautiful song inside it, like: 'Dwelling is not primarily inhabiting, but taking care of and creating that space in which something comes into its own and flourishes.' I even used to go on 'Heideggerian' walks in the woods, ones on which I would be sure to be particularly keen to nature's mysteries. Now there are books out claiming he was anti-Semitic, even though his lover, Hannah Arendt, was Jewish and a fine philosopher in her own right. But I say, so what; if he was, it didn't come out in his work, and what he might have been as a person—whether he was a bigot or a homosexual or a homophobic—doesn't make one jot of difference to his achievement as one of the great thinkers of the twentieth century."

"Speaking of philosophers, I brought you Thomas Berry's *The Dream of the Earth* which you mentioned you'd like to read," Oshanta says.

"Thank you." I stare at the book's cover picture. Although it's a photograph of a stream through a woodland which looks as one might expect, the water appears dreamlike, unreal, changing suddenly from a shimmering unnatural golden color to a startling, turquoise blue. It's beautiful but strangely unsettling.

The landscape is quite different than when I visited here with Oshanta almost a month ago. The trees have now lost all their leaves and the ground has turned from greenish brown to brown. Dark red berries adorn the hawthorn tree. Bertrand reaches up gingerly, cautious of the thorns, plucks a plump bunch and puts one in his mouth.

"My grandmother says one never knows whether the fruit of a hawthorn will be sweet or not; unlike other berries, one can't tell from the color or size or even where the tree is growing. It just has to be tasted. This one's in-between, slightly tart, like a beach plum. Delicious! I wonder if it could be used to make red paint pigments. It would be a terrific, robust red," Bertrand says as he squeezes the juice of one into his palm.

Darth splashes into a pond nearby, making a big enough impression to cause the three mallards idling contently to take flight, quacking with irritation.

As we enter the woodland path, Darth in the lead and me bringing up the rear, I have the strange sensation of having been here recently. Then I remember it had been in the dream of last night; I recall the sound of a flute and Bertrand, Oshanta and I sitting in a circle, and a snake ... then I can't remember anything more, but have that uneasy feeling when you know something bad happened in a dream but can't quite retrieve it, often because you don't really want to experience it again.

We're crossing a small footbridge over a stream. Down along a mossy bank, a small brown bird, fairly non-descript, is flitting quickly about.

The Last Resort

"A winter wren," Bertrand says excitedly. "I've only seen one once before. There were quite a few in these parts at one time, according to early records. But now they're rare, mostly due to the severe reduction of habitat."

"Maybe when we get our land back and then bring back the streams, the winter wrens will return," Oshanta says.

Overhead we hear the call of a red-tailed hawk, as Oshanta and I had on our last hike here together. But this time, his cry sounds different; instead of the quick "kee-kee," followed after a couple of seconds by another, the cry continues over and over, as if it's trying to warn us of something. We all look to the sky. Strange, the sky didn't look this gray a short ways back. We look around us. Rather than smelling the ground as he usually does, Darth sniffs the air excitedly.

"It's fire. The smell of fire," Bertrand says with solemn alarm.

We walk faster, Bertrand and Oshanta nearly running. Ahead we begin to see a mist of smoke becoming as thick as dense fog farther beyond. All the smaller trees and brush are either badly burned or turned to ashes. We come to the high plateau and clearing of the Montauk Indian village. It appears untouched, the tall golden grass whispering in the wind and the hawthorn tree entangled with vines reigning in its burdened majesty over the center of the site. But to the south, we look out on more scorched landscape, extending about a quarter of a mile. To the north, the land appears unharmed. To the west, the direction we came from, and the east, the burning cut only a short distance into the perimeter of the scrub and woodland.

From the center, where not long ago I witnessed the extraordinary moment in which Oshanta's ancestors spoke powerful words of poetry to her, we scan the bleakness around us in silence, except for a low, wounded-animal sound coming from Bertrand. I understand now why hell is portrayed as a place of burning: there's nothing that seems to kill more thoroughly, nothing that appears more opposite from alive than something that's been burned—the blackness of it, the once solid thing that took untold years to grow, in the span of no more than an hour or so reduced to the near insubstance of ashes. I remember an incident from my childhood that upset me for a long time: finding one of my favorite spots—a small grove of white pines that formed a perfect, sanctuary-like circle, where I'd walk with my dog and sometimes camp out or just sit on the soft needled ground and listen to the wind sing its slightly eerie song through the branches—scorched, the trunks of the pines charred half-way up and some even more, the lower branches shriveled to little ugly stumps. How sad—I even cried—and angry I was at the unknown careless beings who could not see what I thought should have been obvious to anyone, that this was a spot of special power and beauty, a sacred spot.

Last night's dream is coming back to me. The half-man half-coyote who ...

"This is not an accident. It's the work of Marshall Kincaid and the commissioner. Kincaid filled in the hole, there, where they had dug the test well, as he said they had when we saw him at the restaurant that day, Paul. But I knew he was lying when he said they had given up because they didn't find water. What they did was clear the underbrush and small trees instead of cutting them—it's easier, more efficient and they can make it look like an accident, if they want. This sets the stage for the golf course they want to build. They left alone the land to the north, because it has more hardwoods than to the south, plus it has popular hiking trails that go around Big Reed Pond that people would make a big fuss about if taken away. Perhaps they also figured by leaving the village here intact we also would not make a big fuss, but they are very mistaken," Oshanta's voice trembles, it sounds as much from anger as sorrow, "for all of this land, not just this site, is important to us."

"This reminds me of old pictures I've seen of the land when it was burned for grazing cattle," Bertrand says in dazed, far-away voice. "At one time, one could see clear to the ocean from here, all grazing land for the cattle. When our people dwelled here, before the settlers began cutting the forest for building their houses and grazing their animals, it was mostly wooded with oaks and beeches, walnut and hickory."

I continue to stare at the blackness before me, as if I'm not really seeing what I'm seeing, as if I'm in a dream.

"Paul, are you all right?" I feel a hand on my arm and jump slightly, surprised.

"It's just that ... " I stop myself, reluctant to admit I dreamt this happening, as if I were an evil conjurer of sorts. Words come from somewhere, urging to be heard: " ... *Voices of the past and of the future who fan these flames of desire and fear, threatening to consume you. You must walk through them, let them burn you if they may, But do not, do not run away."*

"What are those words from?" Oshanta asks, her eyes widening.

"I'm not sure."

"They seem meant for me, for my people—voices of the men in the past who had burned this area, and who now set fire to it again in their unending desire for this land, and who try to instill a fear in us that will consume us. And then, the other voices from the past: my ancestors and my Great Aunt, telling me, for the future of our people, not to be afraid, not to run away."

Oshanta looks far into my eyes, searching for the place the words came from.

"Now I remember. They were from a dream, and you were the one who spoke them to me."

It feels as if we are touching somewhere beyond seeing, beyond the physical. Still staring into the smoldering distance and still in that far-away voice, Bertrand says, "Each of us has his own fires of fear and desire to walk through."

The Dream of the Earth

Journal entry, November 25:
My inner landscape has turned gray and bleak, a mirror of what my eyes have seen. Even looking out at the ocean can't lift my spirits. So many forces outside our control, cutting us down, vanquishing our spirit. We arise in the morning brimming with a sense of possibility, each moment possessing within it the character of a moment of vision, and then at the end of the day, that horizon of being full of light and promise has turned to a dim and featureless land in which life has no meaning, no future.

Gazing off to the facing page of my journal, I notice an entry dated November 20 entitled "Dream of Fire and Wind." I read: *Don't be afraid. You don't understand that we come to tear away the veil ... The wind alone unravels you, filling you with fear, of the wide emptiness now you feel so near.* Oshanta's words as the Wind Spirit in my dream; she knows these winds that "fan the flames" are there "to tear away the veil," the veil that covers the truth, be it joyous or sad, hideous or beautiful. And this is why, rather than feeling defeated by the fire today, Oshanta was like the phoenix arising from the ashes. I pick up the pen again.

Even when the bad seems totally unreasonable or absolutely wrong, we must try to find the hidden gift within it—the gift to our "becoming," as Heidegger says. But we must remember that whatever has been suffered in walking through those flames may not matter at all, except to ourselves. Is this the emptiness we fear that seeps into those dark, silent cracks in our lives—that what we do doesn't matter, that even the whole of our lives might not even matter? Oh, to live as if the moment of the doing matters, and intensely so, but not the moment after—like a bird gliding gleefully on a breeze, though a fierce storm is brewing just to the east, like a gleaming fish reveling in its swim down the stream, though a treacherous current rips right ahead.

As I close my journal, Darth looks up at me. Whenever I finish whatever I'm doing, even if it creates hardly a sound, he knows. Understanding a dog is not even simple.

And then what we think we understand about a dog is only from a human point of view. I'm reminded of my story, about George and Druid, which I haven't worked on in a while. But my mind feels too unfocused to attempt that now. I pick up the book next to me, *The Dream of the Earth*, Oshanta lent me this morning.

"Our secular, rational, industrial society, with its amazing scientific insight and technological skills, has established the first radically anthropocentric society and has hereby broken the primary law of the universe, the law of the integrity of the universe ... The vast mythic, visionary, symbolic world with its all-pervasive numinous qualities was lost. Because of this loss, we made our terrifying assault upon the earth ... Such treatment of the external physical world could not long avoid also encompassing the human. Thus we have the vastest paradox of all—ourselves as free, intelligent, numinous beings negating those very qualities by our own objective reasoning processes and subserving our own rationalizations.

"Western religious traditions have been so occupied with redemptive healing of a flawed world that they tend to ignore creation as it is experienced in our times ... We seldom get to our functional role within the creative intentions of the universe ...

"The American Indian, on the other hand, is the living exemplification of recent understanding of the collective unconscious ... In their traditional mystique of the earth, they are emerging as our surest guides to a viable future ... to call the civilized world back to a more authentic mode of being."

I recall it was after my dream "Fire and Wind" that I first began to perceive Oshanta as a kind of spiritual guide sent to me. I remember the conversation she and I had under the hawthorn tree about Christianity and how it has fostered a schism in our psyches, between the rational/intellectual and the creative/spiritual, and that because of the concept of redemption, instead of appreciating what is, as Native Americans and other traditional peoples tend to do, we are always longing for "what isn't." I think of Bertrand's paintings with their hero and journey symbols and their design around a central symbol. Excited, I read on:

"The excitement of life is in the numinous experience wherein we are given to each other in that larger celebration of existence in which all things attain their highest expression, for the universe is a single, gorgeous celebratory event."

I read this sentence over a couple of times, finding the phrasing particularly felicitous: "...wherein we are given to each other in that larger celebration"—those rare moments when we feel part of us joins with something beyond ourselves, connecting us like tissues of the same body, when life is fecund with meaning and we know we're not alone.

A wave of creative energy surges through me—to write a poem, play the trumpet, something. I pick up my writing notebook, re-read from the beginning the story I'd begun, and start to write, the words seeming to flow from me like the wake from a surfboard cutting through a wave.

> *It's as if the fire had melted away something stuck inside George, shifting his way of seeing things 180 degrees. Druid turned his gaze from the fire to George. He sensed something was different, maybe saw it in the sudden light reflected in his master's blue eyes that most of the time looked as if clouds floated in them.*
>
> *"You know what, boy? I think the time has come to have us a little adventure. I think I'm goin' go see a rhino in the wild,*

see it for Helen. I know it'll make her happy. What we'll do is take a steamer over, or maybe one of those freighters they say you can hitch a ride on, one where I can take you with me. Stop at some islands on the way. Come on, you ready for that walk now?"

Druid jumped up wagging his tail exuberantly. As George opened the door, a wind blew in re-igniting the dwindling fire, making the flicker become a flame.

Tearing Away the Veil

The phone wakes me from a deep sleep. I see it's only seven in the morning.

"Hey, man," I hear on the other end, "this is Brent. Sorry if I'm callin' you too early, but just heard the wave report and the surf's supposed to be good today. The winds are going to change around noon and get nasty though, so we should go out no later than nine, nine-thirty. You up for it?"

"I'm not awake enough yet to think rationally, so I'll say yes. See you here at nine."

Looking out the window, I see the waves forming in even sets and the water's surface turning glassy. I also see some distant cirrus clouds coming in from the west, usually the sign of a storm, so I've learned in reading the sky, while the rising sun is opening its diffuse pink rays to another day. Surfing at nine in the morning on November 26! Now that's pretty interesting, compared to fighting frantic traffic to get to my office downtown, then sitting at a desk and reading over legal papers. A smile stretches across my face; I feel the day opening up to me.

Darth is leading the way down the stairs to the beach, though unable to contain his excitement, he's racing far ahead of us. Off to the east someone's fishing off the rocks. I wonder if it's Captain Lester.

"We'll go out together this time," Brent says as we reach the shoreline. "Waves are about the same height as the last time, but they're fewer and farther between, which makes it easier to paddle out, plus there's less wind than last time, and it's coming from offshore, the most favorable direction. You ready?"

"I think I'm readier than last time. I've worked out a couple of times at the spa you told me about, and have been doing some running, too."

"Good." A wave breaks upon the shore and the water starts receding. "Okay, let's go."

Brent's right—it's not as hard to paddle out this time. The sets being longer, the ebbing sea takes us out quite far without us having to exert as much effort, and we haven't yet encountered another wave. Also, my arms feel stronger and my balance steadier. A wave is almost upon me; I lift up the nose of my board at just the right moment and ride smoothly over its top. I look to the east at Brent; he gives me a quick thumbs up. We paddle about another 50 feet.

I like this part almost as much as the ride: the waiting, rolling along quiescently with the waves, your thoughts ranging out freely to the horizon and beyond, though a corner of your eye remains ever vigilant for that singular swell looming in the distance. This sublime tension, between the sea lulling you to beautiful daydreams and your fear and excitement in anticipating a wave, between apparent calmness and hidden power, swirls at the vortex of the sea's lure, a lure that anyone who's spent time on the sea must feel.

Brent signals me to turn my board around. I get ready, glimpse backward and see it coming. It's larger than I imagined. A cold bolt of fear shoots through me. Stay calm.

The wave is breaking to the west, so I should catch it just a few seconds after Brent.

There he goes—okay, one, two, three—now!

My heart leaps straight up into my throat as I'm thrust forward in a juggernaut so fast I feel I'm almost flying through the air, my arms wings and legs a rudder trying to steer me through the swift currents and keep me from tipping into a 90-degree nosedive. I can't believe it, but I'm still vertical. I look to the east, and Brent, about 15 feet away and nearly parallel to me, gives me a smile and thumbs up. No feeling I've ever had comes close to this, except maybe ...

I almost lose my balance. But I do get in front of the wave, ending my ride. I turn around, ready to paddle back out again. Brent sees me and starts to make his way toward me.

"Hey, man, you really did fine. You rode about twice as long as the last time we went out. But, I don't know if we should go out again. The wind is picking up and coming out of the west now, and the waves are getting bigger and choppier. That storm is coming in faster than I expected."

"Just one more? If you don't want to, I think I can manage myself."

"I was only thinking about you, but if you feel you can handle it, fine. As long as the waves are ridable, I could surf all day."

It's a little rougher paddling this time, but at least we're already half-way there. This time I know which one to take without Brent signaling me, and I watch the wave instead of him. Steady—now! A much bumpier ride than the last one; legs have to be springier, reflexes lightning fast. Keep at the right angle. Don't get glued to a spot like a statue, as Brent said. Feet are almost as important as eyes. Sense the wave through the board; translate its motion into your own. Aspire to be as fluid as a wave.

A sudden gust of wind hits me, enough to throw me off my already precarious balance. I plunge into the water, the waves pushing me down, down, around, swallowing me inside of them. I see the light above. Summoning all the strength I have left, I struggle to swim to it, yet, as though I were suddenly thrust into a nightmarish dimension where the opposite of what I expect actually happens, instead of getting closer I'm slipping farther away, the color now changing from dark gray-green to dark gray. A vague face appears behind the sea's now far-above frothy veil. A sign, a sign! But the face fades away. Darkness is closing in rapidly now. A school of small bright fish swims toward me, curious and unafraid.

Little streams of light begin filtering through, as if someone were looking at me with a flashlight from vast reaches of space and time. Opening my eyes wider, I see three faces hovering over me: a young man's, a large man's with a red beard and red hair and one black snout licking my face.

"'Bout time ya come round. Well, guess ya met the ol' Sea Hag that time. Quite a frightening experience, aint it? Now, how many fingers ya see?"

It seems too hard to find words, partly because I'm not completely convinced yet I'm in the world of the living and partly because my stomach feels so upset anything might cause it to wretch.

"Wow, man. Am I ever glad to see your eyes!"

"Come on now fella, how many fingers? We got to know you're okay, or else we better get ya to the hospital lickity split."

My mind beginning to clear, I recognize Brent and the man as Captain Lester and understand his concern. "Two," I manage to mutter.

"Okay, good. Young fella, let's get him to his feet and up to his house. Then he ought to take a warm bath."

They help me to my feet and, on either side of me, support me as I trudge slowly across the beach. My legs feel so rubbery, almost as if they're not part of me. It seems to take forever to ascend the stairs.

"Thanks, Brent and Captain Lester, though that hardly seems adequate for having saved my life."

"Well, I didn't do anything but come over when I saw this young fella pulling ya in. If you'd been under a minute or more, that might have been it for ya. He pumped your chest and gave ya mouth-to-mouth, too."

"Fortunately, I worked as a lifeguard a couple of summers here in Montauk, so I knew what to do."

"I once saved a drunken fisherman who fell overboard. But I don't know if I could have swum out there today against them waves like this fella did. Not quite as swift as I used to be. Then, ya never know what ya might be capable of when it comes to life and death."

"Brent, I hope I can do something to help repay you sometime." I shake his hand and then Captain Lester's. "I think I'm okay now. Oh, before you go, what was that you said about the Sea Hag?"

"That's what us ol' Bonackers call the sea when she gets nasty. We say the sea's pretty as a mermaid, and she lures ya out to her. But you got to be careful not to challenge her too far, go beyond your limits as a man, because she'll turn into the Terrifying Sea Hag, the wind whipping her up into a frenzy making her voice scream through the riggin', her temper turning as mean as the mounting waves. Many a fisherman here's been victim to her, including an uncle and cousin of mine."

"Yes, and Brent tried to warn me, but I didn't want to listen. Thought I could outwit her, I guess."

"Ah, that thinkin will get ya far in the world of men, but in nature it could mean your end."

As I close my eyes and soak in the warm water through to my cold, weary bones, my mind recedes to those darkening moments in the watery depths: the veiled face appearing and disappearing, the feeling of being abandoned and finally the wide-mouthed emptiness swallowing me up. And then ... out of the enclosing darkness, when the glimmering fish were swimming toward me, as if in their unison all of one mind, I became suddenly calm and unafraid. Rather than emptiness, life and its unfathomable mysteries shimmered all around.

Words from Saint Thomas I had read long ago come alive in my mind: "The kingdom of God is spread upon the earth, but man does not see it."

Feeding the Fire

My eyes open to Darth licking my face. It's late afternoon and a deep orange purple sunset is painting itself upon the horizon. As I arise, my body sorely reminds me of the morning's high adventure. The anticipation of seeing Oshanta soon, however, subverts the pain for the moment; she's invited me to her house this evening for the first time.

As I pull up in front of her cabin, a light on the porch appears, the only light in the surrounding darkness into which Oshanta emerges.

"Paul, welcome to my little shack in the woods."

"Thank you for inviting me."

The first thing I notice: Oshanta's brown eyes have a golden glint in them tonight, as if containing little flames, but though her eyes sparkle and shine, her face and smile have a subdued, slightly sad and wistful look. She is wearing a black top, like a dancer's top, that reveals her beautiful neck, the first time I've ever seen it.

She reaches down to pick up some wood stacked near the door. "The fire needs replenishing."

"Please, allow me."

I follow her into the house. The design is exactly the same as Olivia's and Bertrand's houses: the small kitchen opening into the dark beamed living room with a stone hearth on one side. Against the east wall a day bed looks out through a large arched window onto the harbor. A round table with two candles upon it and a few chairs around it presides over the middle of the room, and facing the fireplace sits a couch with a slate table in front of it. The wood walls are lined with photographs, all black and white except for a few.

I kneel, placing a couple of logs on the hearth and the others carefully on top of the fire, in a more or less teepee shape. Watching me, Oshanta covers her mouth in an attempt to hide bemusement, it seems.

"Forgive me for laughing, but the way you make a fire, Paul, seems so ... precise."

"Well, I must confess, I'm trying to learn how to build a good fire, or maybe to relearn, because I did know at one time in my youth. But I remember it took first unlearning the method I'd learned in the Boy Scouts, which was to build a fire in this neat teepee formation, one log at roughly a sixty degree angle against another on top of a specified mass of paper and kindling. The basic form was right, but it needed to be less structured. Strange that activities which by their nature are more instinctual could be more difficult to learn than, say, the binary concepts in computer technology."

"An apt analogy for how far from nature we've wandered, how we tend to approach things from the outside in, from the theoretical to the real, instead of the other way around. Just like the people trying to develop our Indian lands. They're only thinking about what they want, not about the land itself—the people, history and natural history that are all parts of the truth of that piece of land. It would take too much time, and they're in a big hurry."

"Have you found out anything about the fire?"

"Yes. I found out there's an agreement between the State Parks Department and an environmental group, the New York Conservation Society, to conduct experimental controlled burns in New York State parks, and this was one of the first experiments. The idea is to burn the non-native brush that has taken over to make room for the native grasses and other plants to thrive again, a technique which was used in the past and which the land and plant life became adapted to and dependent upon for proper regrowth. The park ranger, Mr. Fithian, assured me they'd had an agreement on the books for over a year now, and that they'd actually planned to burn earlier in the fall, but the weather was never right on the particular days they'd set. So, wanting to get it in before winter, the day before Thanksgiving was the day it finally happened."

Still kneeling, I take a poker from the side of the hearth and loosen the logs from each other a bit. Bright new flames leap to life. "What do you think?"

"Well, I have read that prescribed burns are now a land management tool being tried out west and in other areas, for just the reasons, and others, Mr. Fithian mentions. After all, my people introduced the white settlers to controlled burning—to clear land for farming. But then the settlers did it on a larger scale, for raising livestock. Aren't modern white settlers, in the form of multi-national companies, still doing this in South American and other rain forests? Anyway, I also made a call to the Conservation Society, to see if they have an ongoing agreement with the State to monitor the area they burned, which actually might be something positive to come out of all this, because it would imply that the State wouldn't have other plans for it, such as for a golf course. The director told me they're going to monitor the progress of the native plant communities, and that they were not aware of any other plans for the area by the State.

"She said that a golf course would be absolutely in conflict with what they're trying to accomplish, even if the plant communities in question could be successfully protected from encroachment, because of the drain on the aquifer and the pollution of the aquifer from golf course fertilizers. However, she said now golf course builders are becoming 'environmentally friendly' by planning courses that use little water and no fertilizers, like the links courses of England and Scotland. Even the Audubon Society supposedly has some literature out praising the new approach. This area would lend itself to such a course. Then, once they put in the first fairways where they burned, they might get bold and extend northward toward the dunes and Block Island Sound, with some scenic water holes."

"Maybe, in addition to the golf course, they're thinking of making it into a theme park kind of place, turn the park office where Mr. Fithian is into a colonial inn for dining and rooms. It could be a very successful venture," I add. The golden flames of Oshanta's eyes seem to spark.

"And maybe they'd like to dress up the Indians in feathers and beaded deerskins to add to the ambiance. Build a little wigwam for us in a little model village. The locals, the majority of whom are tourist-hungry business people, would love the idea of a theme park. Yes. I would be the lone voice in the wilderness. Once it gains momentum, there won't be any way to stop it either, because I won't be able to prove my case for the Montauks' rights to the land for a couple of years, I estimate, at best."

It's the first time I've seen real discouragement in Oshanta's face. The glow in her eyes begins to fade. I sit next to her on the couch and take her hand in mine.

"I feel I'm running out of time, my dream of doing this for my people turning to ashes before my eyes."

Suddenly, the dream I had of Katherine's picture burning in the fire flashes before me, and her words to me: *Feed the fire or the fire will die. I'm sorry I never told you this.* I squeeze Oshanta's hand, reflexively. She turns her eyes toward me.

"There's still time," I say with an intensity that takes Oshanta by surprise. "What about those legislators in Albany who said they'd try to help you?"

"They said they inquired into any plans for this park by the Parks Department, and were told nothing was going on. They've given me letters to the Bureau of Indian Affairs supporting our investigation into our land claim. But beyond that, there's not much more they can do at this point. The burn seems to have been legitimate, the well-drilling has stopped, and nothing has been disturbed at the actual Montaukett village site. And as far as we know, no 'proposed project' exists."

"Perhaps not, but there's probably a paper trail of some kind. Someone just has to find it—a hungry reporter or a lawyer. And I know just the one: a friend of mine who works in Albany on the Governor's staff. I'll give him a call tomorrow, okay?"

"Thank you. I'm sorry for being so despairing. It's not like me."

"There's nothing to be sorry about—even the most indomitable spirits are allowed to get down once in a while. And besides, I'm glad you can be whatever way you feel with me." I turn my face toward the fire. "What is to be sorry about is that one can be with someone for years and hide his or her disappointments and despairs, as if those parts of life were only to be suffered alone. What I've also discovered—a little late, I'm afraid—is that our emotions seem to have an internal symmetry which operates below our level of awareness, so that when we deny sharing the sad parts, the truly joyful moments become lost to us as well."

Oshanta looks from my face into the fire. "An interesting thought and I think probably true." She looks back at me, her eyes wide, scanning my face as if trying to recognize who I am, and also maybe who I was. I'm afraid I've said too much. I hope she doesn't ask me questions because I'm not ready, no, not ready to talk about Katherine. Work, okay, but not Katherine.

"I remember the first time I came to your house when we were talking about the sensibilities of the artist as opposed to the lawyer, and you said you were trying to develop 'the other' sensibility. It seems to me, in the short time I've known you, you've changed."

Relieved, I laugh a bit nervously. "Sometimes I don't even recognize myself anymore. I've had more interesting thoughts since I've been out here and feel so much more creative than ever before, not in the sense of producing anything as much as in just *living*. In the city it seems we get so caught up with having to produce something tangible to prove our worth—what do you do, what are you doing, what have you done?—that the fun is often taken out of being creative. The end-result is what becomes more important than the doing."

"Exactly," Oshanta says excitedly. "That's one of the reasons I moved out here part-time. I've done more *good* photography since I've been here, though I've not done that much of it. I've also been spending more time doing documentary photographing, of the Montauk lands and my people. Ironically, it has felt more creative than much of the 'artistic' work I've done, I think because it has involved me more completely—not just intellectually or theoretically. It's made me realize being creative is something broader and deeper than I had ever thought. As you said before, it has more to do with how you approach your life, which is how native peoples traditionally think of creativity, too. In their view, if you're living a certain way, in accordance with certain principles, then you're able to awaken to the spirit of creativity in yourself and in all things; thus your *life*, rather than an isolated act here and there, becomes creative."

"I'm reminded of a wonderful line in the Thomas Berry book you lent me: 'The excitement of life is in the numinous experience wherein we are given to each other in that larger celebration of existence in which all things attain their highest expression ...'" Smiling, a golden light illuminating her eyes again, she takes my hand and brushes the back of it against her cheek, its warmth seeping through to my palm and fingertips. Sublime—how strange and exciting to feel this word that rarely seems true beyond a book's page. A tingling sensation spreads under my skin and inside my head.

"I'm afraid I'm being a negligent host. I should get us some wine and check on the dinner."

"And while you're doing that, I'd like to look at your photographs."

"Of course. Most of them are fairly recent and relate to my project with my people. They may not be my professional best, but I guess I'd call them my personal best."

I recognize the face of Oshanta's Aunt Olivia. She is smiling that benevolent and wise-Buddha kind of smile, her eyes dancing with fire as when I first met her. Her face, which takes up about three-quarters of the picture, is imposed upon a background that looks to be the Montauk village site with the remains of a stone wall and a hawthorn tree in bloom. The bottom half of the background is landscape and the top half a sweep of cloudless sky. The light is rich and warm, and both photos are done in a sepia tone enhancing their richness and feeling of authenticity.

Next to it is another similar composition, though Olivia's face is quite the opposite in demeanor: in the same sepia tone, it has that solemn, sad cast that one finds in many classic Edward Curtis photographs of Native Americans, but without a romanticized aura. In Olivia's eyes and face I see, not hurt masked with dignity, but bewilderment—"how can people be this way to other people"—and also challenge—"I'm not going to stand idly by or drown myself in pessimism." In the background, in black and white rather than sepia, is a photo of the village site that Oshanta took recently with the men in hard hats and the water drilling rig.

Bertrand is the subject of the next series of sepia-toned and black and white close-up portraits; there're also some seascapes of him in his clamming boat, just as I first saw him. The sense of light is bold, starkly contrasting with the dark elements, reminding me of the awe-filled light that Ansel Adams achieved in his work, and that I liked so much in the nineteenth century landscape painters I had collected.

A large portrait of Samson dominates the center of the next composition on the wall. In his church vestments, he's standing in front of an altar, his hands folded in prayer, head bent forward and eyes closed. This black and white image is superimposed on a larger photograph, also black and white, of a crucifix, and at each of its four points is a biblical saying in calligraphic writing: "Deliver us from evil," "Love thy neighbor," "God, why hast thou forsaken me?" "He maketh me lie down in green pastures." In the background is a montage of sepia-toned historical drawings; in the upper left side is a drawing of a Native American shaking hands with a colonist, underneath which are the words in calligraphic writing "Wyandanch and Gardiner, 1600s: the beginning of the end"; in the upper right is a photograph of an elderly woman standing in front of a lighthouse and smiling wearily, underneath which is written "Queen Maria"; a drawing of a judge in a courtroom full of Native Americans with the words underneath "Judge Blackmar, 1909, Denies Existence of Montauks" appears in the bottom left side; and on the bottom right, a photograph of Stephen Pharaoh holding a walking stick, underneath which is written his name.

Oshanta approaches and hands me a glass of wine. "My first true photo montage. I'm not yet comfortable with it. It seems gimmicky. But on the other hand, I can achieve an effect and relay a message that is much more complex than in a single image."

"I think it's very powerful. The others are too, but, as you say, this is more complicated."

"Yes, and ambiguous, which I'm not sure is a good thing. One can see it as a message of hope, that through prayer, belief in Christ, and the words of the Bible, all people who have been sinned against, as well as those who have sinned, can find salvation and forgiveness, which is how Samson would probably see it; another might see in it not only the uselessness of Christianity to change people's evil ways, but its hypocrisy; that in the name of Christianity and fighting evil heathenism, white men came and conquered the Indian savages with the arrogance of 'saving them from themselves,' just as they subdued their wild kingdom into fenced and tamed green pastures, and then took it for themselves. How do you see it?"

"The latter way—I don't see how a white American could understand it any other way, really. An image like this reopens that deep wound of guilt we still carry of what we did, and are still doing to some extent, to the Native Americans. Of course, some have buried that wound effectively, and they might look at this and be confused and irritated. But underneath they would know the truth."

"I wonder if that wound will ever heal, on either side. Samson likes to think it will, but I don't believe it, as long as there are Indian sites where nuclear wastes are dumped, our bones plowed up and golf courses built."

"And do you think this prevents Native Americans from truly trusting white Americans?"

"I think whoever we are we can only learn to trust people one at a time."

I take her hand in mine, slowly, a little nervously. "Yes, you're right. Well, for my part, I feel closer to you than I have to anyone in a very long time, and I've only known you for such a short while. It's kind of amazing to me, really."

She turns her face toward me, her golden eyes slightly misty, her neck, so alluring. I want to feel its perfect contours with my fingertips. Ah, so smooth, so excitingly yet comfortingly warm. Palms move down over her shoulders. She closes her eyes as I close mine.

Pieces of the poem by Yeats that Katherine most liked to read aloud, suddenly speak to me, in a voice that sounds at once familiar and completely new.

> *I went out to the hazel wood, because a fire was in my head ... dropped a berry in a stream and caught a little silver trout. When I laid it on the floor I went to blow the fire aflame ... someone called me by my name. It had become a glittering girl ... who ran and faded through the brightening air. Though I am old with wandering ... I will find out where she has gone and kiss her lips and take her hands ... and pluck till time and times are done ... the golden apples of the sun."*

Voices of the Past and of the Future

I awake in a sweat. Erotic, strange, sometimes violent dreams of Katherine—making love to Katherine, Katherine burning in a fire, Katherine swimming in the ocean then changing into a glittering fish and swimming out to sea.

I look out my bedroom window. The first light of day is peeking over the water, illuminating the white crests of waves as they appear then disappear. Once in a while, when not enough time has elapsed between the approaching and receding waves, they collide, often quite spectacularly, in a foamy clash; just as Oshanta and Katherine—the approaching and receding waves—collided in my dream last night.

Words from "Wandering Angus" drift through my mind again. Could it be Katherine is trying to warn me not to let this new glittering girl disappear through the brightening air? Have I confused a fear of losing love with a fear of finding it?

I look out through the window again. The sun is now emerging above the long blue line: Oshanta, the bright sun rising, Katherine the nostalgic blue horizon line stretching endlessly in both directions. Is love something that has no beginning or end—the feeling when I first saw Katherine that I already loved her and now, that I always will? Or can it come and go, like the crests of these waves, like the fading stars in the brightening air?

The sensation I've felt before, of being caught in a gravityless space between time moving forward and time moving backward, no sense of here, no sense of me—as if I'm composed of no more than the empty air around me—billows through me like a fog.

I wish I could speak to Katherine—no. What could I say? What could she say? There's nothing to say.

I pick up my trumpet next to the bed and start blowing a few notes. Just think about each sound, try to link them together in a pleasing way. Yes, that's better. Close my eyes. Imagine Oshanta and Katherine like beautiful clouds above the sea, Oshanta floating off to the east and Katherine to the west. To the west, where the spirits of those departed live, whispering words of poetry. But beware: don't linger long on these voices of the past lest you miss the sweet sound of the future passing by on an awakening east wind.

Hither Woods

I hang up the phone with my friend Bob Messinger in Albany. Anxious to tell Oshanta about my conversation, I dial her number. No answer.

"I know. You up for an adventure, Darth?" It's about eight miles to Oshanta's house from here, so I figure we'll take the car about half-way, a little past town, and hike the rest. She might be home by then, and if she's not, we'll have had a good hike. Need to pick up some supplies in town, too.

A brisk, sunny, late fall day. One can almost feel the coming coldness in the air and life bending inward, hunkering down. I pass by the Japanese pines at the beginning of town, withering and turning brown from what Oshanta has told me is caused by a disease attacking many of these trees in the area. As a non-native specie, it's vulnerable. Yet some alien species thrive, even aggressively supplant indigenous species, she said, as the phragmites reed often have the native cattail reed which now is quite rare in this part of the world, and in fact Big Reed Pond near the Montauk Village site has one of the largest remaining stands in the whole Northeast. The phragmites/cattail story is an apt analogy in the plant world to what happened in the human world between the white settlers and her people, she added, and, generally, between white people and indigenous peoples everywhere.

We're coming to a long stretch of oak forest. I recall wondering on my frenzied ride out here a month ago why these trees appeared not terribly tall and all the same height. In reading a short historical account of this area, known as Hither Woods, I've learned that a huge fire raged through here about 20 years ago burning most of the trees about half-way down. Owned jointly by the State, County of Suffolk and Town of East Hampton, the land was afterwards preserved from development primarily because a large source of potable water exists in its ground, Oshanta informed me, and Montauk depends solely on such sources for its drinking water.

A large map of the park stands at the edge of the woods. There's a trail running parallel to the road that ends in the Walking Dunes on the east side of Napeague Harbor, across the water from Oshanta's house. When we drove by here on our way to her aunt's house, Oshanta told me that Stephen Talkhouse Pharaoh, the Montaukett famous for his walking—from Montauk to Brooklyn in a day, legend has it, to earn two bits to deliver a message—and whose walking stick she inherited at Thanksgiving dinner, had lived in these woods in a small hut. One would notice some stone remains in a circular formation, somewhat off the path.

Interspersed between the oak we come upon some robust American beech, mountain laurel so large as to appear like trees and tall hollies probably of a considerable age, all spared by the fire. Darth, eagerly sniffing and darting about, is obviously thrilled with the change of smell and scene from ocean/dunes to woodland with its enticing scents of rabbits, deer and, as I too have suddenly detected, fox. It's the kind of woods I remember as a child: thick, hushed, dark and deep enough to be a kingdom onto itself, a veritable Sherwood Forest where one can hide from the rest of the world.

In the midst of this green and brown world stands a stark stunted tree bleached gray-white like old bones, a ghostly reminder of the fire's intensity. Since it's still standing, does it only appear to be dead, a small heart of life yet beating in its hollow? Perched atop the highest branch like a winged messenger poised between the world of the living and the dead, a large crow surveys its domain. A ray of sunlight reveals a shimmer of blue in his black wings, flexed and ready for sudden fortuitous flight. In his raspy voice, he emits a cautionary and proprietary caw-caw.

Words of Stephen Pharaoh that Oshanta spoke in Indian Fields suddenly come to me: *"So many miles of earth did I walk, through dark, quiet woods and sunlit fields, so like good friends we became that I know with the power to talk they would say 'Tread more lightly upon me, I pray.'"* I imagine his tall, lithe body moving through this woods 100 or so years ago, knowingly and somehow noiselessly, despite the crisp autumn leaves underfoot. An ancestor of this crow would not bother to comment upon his passing underneath, so much a part of the woods was he.

Making my way along a curved ridge, I gaze into the hollow below. Almost obscured by the reddish brown leaves covering the ground, a few rounded gray-white stones form part of a circle. Without foreknowledge this was once a dwelling, a passerby would never know. It seems a strange spot to choose for one's dwelling: this tiny hollow engulfed by dense looming oaks extending for miles in every direction. I climb down the ridge and stand in the middle of what would have been the house. Now I see. The trees, rather than overwhelming, are like great arms hugging this small space, protecting it from extremes of weather and, perhaps more importantly for its inhabitant, from the prying eyes of those from Out There beyond the edge of this friendlier world.

And how unfriendly that world Out There was to young Stephen Pharaoh when, due to the desperate poverty of his family, he was sold to his mother's employer, a Colonel Parsons of East Hampton, for $40—a dollar a pound! (I hadn't known that Indians were bought and sold as slaves until Oshanta told me this story.) Unable to endure such a state of indentureship, he soon ran away to sea on a whaling ship. Not only did he manage to survive, in a profession in which many Montauks lost their lives, but apparently thrived. From cabin boy he became mate, and when offered the command, legend has it he refused saying he did not want to command white men.

Much more adventurous than others of his tribe, Stephen found his way to California where he prospected for gold, eventually wandering back east where he fought with a Connecticut regiment in the Civil War. Afterwards, he returned to Montauk where he made a living like most other Indians did: as a guide for white hunters and fishermen and selling ice he'd cut from ponds in the winter. Of all his myriad occupations and talents, the one he seems most remembered for is his ability to walk great distances at almost inhuman speeds. In fact, so well-known did he become for this gift that he was hired as a champion race-walker in the Barnum and Bailey Circus.

When the Montauks were increasingly forced off their land in Indian Fields in the latter 1800s, dispersing to other parts of East Hampton, Sag Harbor, and as far as Wisconsin where a settlement had begun a century before, Stephen Pharaoh built this dwelling deep in Hither Woods. He fought in the courts and in Albany for the Montauks' land, as others before and after him would, unsuccessfully. As if it were just too much for him to bear, he died in 1879 when all of the land from the eastern edge of Napeague to Montauk Point, about 10,000 acres, was auctioned off to a man named Arthur Benson, owner of the Brooklyn Light and Gas Company, for the incredible sum of $151,000.

As I ponder what living here 100 years ago might have been like, I suddenly realize that what I'm doing is more *pretend,* as if I were a kid dressing up like Robin Hood or Robinson Crusoe. Living like this, like Stephen Pharaoh did, would be the true escape—to live this simply, to know this as the real world, its life forms and pathways, sounds and smells. Though I'm not about to make that much of a change, I do know I already feel so much better not watching TV shows and commercials, not reading newspaper headlines of the next political scandal, and not being exposed to the endless, monotonous marketing of everything so that life loses its depth and color and shape, so that we can't even distinguish what is meaningful and true anymore.

I hear the caw-caw, now like a laugh, of the crow overhead. He knows how much bigger, stronger and truer his world is than mine; he'll survive no matter what happens to us, and he knows, no matter how hard I try, I'll never completely understand his world. But there's no scornful tone in his laugh, rather a playfully mocking, teasing tone, cajoling me further and deeper into knowing his woods. Some words from a favorite Wallace Stevens poem Katherine liked to read, "Thirteen Ways of Looking at a Blackbird," come to me.

> *... I know noble accents*
> *And lucid, inescapable rhythms;*

The Last Resort

*But I know, too,
That the blackbird is involved
In what I know.
When the blackbird flew out of sight,
It marked the edge
Of one of many circles ...*

Setting out on the trail again, soon we come to the edge of the woods and find ourselves in a vast white landscape that stretches as far as my eye can see, interrupted only occasionally with black pines, dwarf oaks and silvery shad. Like the dunes I'd explored closer to my house, they're also in the shape of waves, though much larger—maybe 30 to 40 feet high.

After walking a ways, I feel the wind getting stronger, see the sand shifting, lifted from one dune to begin building another, grain by grain. I find a twig and stick it in the sand. After only a minute, at least a quarter-inch of sand has been blown away: The Walking Dunes. How wonderful, and slightly eerie, it is to see geological time happening right before my eyes. I imagine I'm in a swirling white time machine, fast forwarding to the future, and that the wind could blow me away too, atom by atom, recreating me in another form in another time and place. But when I try to picture myself in the future, I'm surprised I hit an impenetrable wall. Where I *can* picture myself is in the past, about 100 years ago.

With my arm around Darth's neck, I tuck my head down, the wind now so strong, and glance quickly off to the north. Beyond a great valley carved through the dunes shines the dark wintry blue of Gardiner's Bay.

Finally leaving the dunes, we come to the east side of Napeague Harbor. The sand here is an unusual rust color, similar to that of the bluffs along the ocean beach where my house is, caused by the high content of iron in the groundwater, Oshanta has told me. Scattered along the tide line, jingle shells of shimmery light orange and pale yellow hues, along with scallop and muscle shells of iridescent purple-blue, create a harmonious mosaic against the orange sand. Why is it that no matter how facile or imaginative the painter, he can never quite create the exact colors of nature? In spite of a brain that can calculate complex mathematical equations that send people to the moon and beyond, and that has mapped the human genome, we still can't do many things that nature can, even recreating the pale yellow of a jingle shell.

We come to Oshanta's house. I knock on the door; no answer, though her car is parked in the drive. Perhaps she's next door at her aunt's. We walk there and before I knock, Oshanta opens the door. Her face is the most solemn I've ever seen it.

"Hello, Paul. Olivia is not at all well. The cold she got before Thanksgiving has turned into pneumonia, I think. But she won't call a doctor because she's afraid he'll put her in the hospital and she doesn't want to go. She believes her time has come, and she wants to stay here. I've called the rest of the family. They'll be here soon. Bertrand had gone to the city today and will be coming back tonight."

"I'm so sorry."

"Why don't you come in."

"Are you sure?"

"Yes. I think she'd like to see you."

She is lying in her bed with her head propped up looking out the window of her bedroom to the harbor. Her hair isn't braided upon her head as it had been on previous occasions, but loose and flowing. I'm amazed at how thick and long it is, for a woman of her age, and with only thin streaks of gray. Her face has the same slightly smiling, slightly sad expression as when I first saw her by the fireside in the other room, though new lines of strain are evident.

"Hello, Olivia."

"Hello, Paul," she says without looking at me. She recognizes the sound of my voice. "You've been in the woods. I smell oak leaves and pine needles. One of the only senses I have that still works passably well." She laughs faintly. Her voice has half the liveliness it had before. "Tell me, where were you and what did you see?"

"I was in Hither Woods. I saw where Stephen Pharaoh lived and thought about him, from what Oshanta has told me about his life. I saw a crow, and thought about how he and Stephen Pharaoh probably understood each other in some way, and how I'll never be able to understand a crow in that way. It seems a wonderful knowledge to have—of the woods, its creatures, of a world that has been lost to most of us, so busy are we with creating our own world. It's interesting to imagine: if we had been receptive to what your people knew instead of trying to destroy you when we arrived on your shores, what a different culture would have evolved in this country."

"Maybe, maybe not. Remember, there was much that was wrong with our people, too. Tribes tried to destroy other tribes—out of greed for territory, for food. Though the Montauks were not warlike, our neighbors to the north, the Pequots in Connecticut and the Narragansett in Rhode Island, were. They were jealous of us: the Manito of the sea gave us more quahogs off our shores for making wampum than he gave them. But it is true most of this warring happened after white men arrived, especially after they massacred Pequots in the early 1600s in the Pequot War causing some tribes like the Montauks to side with the English just to protect themselves from being slaughtered, too. The sad and bitter truth is that we gave the settlers rights to our land in return for their help in protecting us from the bloody raids of the Pequots and Narragansett, not understanding that the settlers would then think of the land as belonging only to them. "So, it is not just white man but Man who must change. And a powwaw understands this; he sees beyond his own small circle of people into the larger one of Man and then the even larger one of the spirits, as Black Elk did in his vision of the many hoops of the world, and as Stephen Pharaoh did, too. This is why he did not hate white men, in spite of what they had done. This is also why he could understand the crow."

"He didn't see himself, in some essential way, as better than the crow," I say.

"My people saw animals and all of nature as being more powerful than man, which kept us in a proper relationship. The crow is a sacred bird to us. In our mythology, Conconchus the crow was a messenger sent by the god of creation, Cautanowwit, to deliver corn, our most important food, and beans to us. Powwaws could have moments of being this powerful, when their spirits could take flight into a higher realm, join with the greater spirits and then return with a vision to help others see, but these were only moments. And these visions were often achieved by becoming like the bear, the wolf, the eagle or the wind."

"Or like a glowing ember in the fire of life."

Olivia smiles faintly. "You remembered. Well, it is said Stephen Pharaoh had a kind of glow about him, even when he was young—not a hot-tempered, fast-burning glow, but the kind from a fire that's been burning for a while and just makes you feel good and peaceful near it no matter how bad you felt before. And I remember seeing it in the face of my grandmother Queen Maria when she was reaching her last years on this earth. Somehow they were able to go beyond the flames of anger and disappointment that consume most of us, to find some important truth and peace. Maybe if I'd had a little more time ..."

Her voice trails off. I look at Oshanta, a tear falling from her eye. Olivia stares out the window with that sad yet smiling expression. A cloud passes over the dark blue water.

"But it's silly to think like that. The Manitos know better than me. And what does my little life matter anyway? It is like a cloud passing by that soon disappears to become part of the big sky. I'll be happy to join Stephen Pharaoh, Queen Maria, Pocahontas and all of the ancestors above where it is said days are always warm and food plentiful. And as we sit around our great fire in the sky, we'll watch over Runs with the Wind, Bertrand and Samson and smile. Then maybe one night you'll look up and see a new star like a glowing ember in the western sky."

Like a Glowing Ember

A bright orange sun is sinking in the western sky over Lake Montauk as we climb the last few feet to the top of the hill. We look out to water and sky in every direction. A simple white picket fence defines a small area of ground, in the middle of which stands a white marble headstone with "Stephen Talkhouse Pharaoh, Civil War Veteran, 1819 -1879" etched on it. Other graves of Montauketts are marked with no more than a few stones. It's not a custom of Native Americans to erect tombstones, Oshanta whispers to me, and the one for Stephen Pharaoh was given by the government in honor of his military service.

Silently we gather in a circle just inside the fence and then everyone starts to hold hands. Oshanta is on one side of me and an older woman I'd never met on the other. My palm feels the lines etched in hers. She holds my hand as if she's known me for a long time.

Samson begins speaking in his deep and musical voice.

We gather here to bid you a fond farewell
and good tidings for your journey to the life beyond this.
We're also here to give our last thanks for the many joys
and teachings you've imparted to us.
Your speaking of my great ancestor Reverend Samson
Occum and your own deep sense of the world of the spirit

I know were the keys to unlocking what I was to become.
We now will vow to keep the promises we gave.
I'll build the school you wanted on our land someday.
This small wooden replica I made of that future school I
now give to you.

Samson steps forward and places the wooden model inside the pine box, then says,

'Oh eternity, eternity! Who can measure it? Who can count
the years thereof, arithmetic must fail.

"Those were words from a eulogy by Reverend Samson Occum in 1772, words that allude to his belief in The Great Awakening, that we will be reborn eternally until we shed all our sins. To me, they speak of our eternal striving in this world, to become one with the Great Spirit, with God. Olivia, you were an example for all of us in this striving, as you will be for generations to come."

Samson returns to the circle and Oshanta walks forward.

There is so much you've given to me
I can't possibly begin to name everything.
But the most important gift
is the knowledge of what I was meant to be.
Like a fish the tide had swept in,
I was floundering there on the edge of the sea when you
found me and showed me
a truer way to be.
This very place upon which we stand,
our sacred burial ground,
you showed me how to save from
being carelessly destroyed.
I deeply regret I couldn't fulfill all your dreams before you
went on,
but I promise you I'll not stop until I succeed
in returning our land to its proper hands.
I give you a copy of the 1687 deed I'll use in my fight,

that guarantees forever Montauks and their heirs rights to their land.
May the Great Spirit be always with you.
And may your great spirit be always with us.

Oshanta steps forward and places the paper in the box. She returns to the circle.

The silence extends beyond a minute or so. Everyone expects Bertrand to deliver the next eulogy, but Olivia's death has been very hard on him. He's not spoken more than a few words in the couple of days since it happened.

Finally, he walks forward slowly, reaches inside a backpack and pulls out a small framed painting.

Because my hands can express more what I feel
I give you this painting in gratitude,
and also so that part of me can always be by your side.
It's an image of you as you wished to be but did not know was already true.
A painting of a fire from whose orange-red flames arises a beautiful woman with the wings of a crow.
The wood burning in the fire is the symbol of Man,
as according to Montauk legend the God of Creation Cautanowwit
created man from the wood of a tree.
And when the wood has burned down to warm glowing embers,
the best and purest of Man is what's left
and ascends into the realm of spirit energy.
With the wings of the crow
you also represent the messenger of Cautanowwit
sent to give us what we need to know.
Know now that you were, are and will be that ember in the fire that will forever glow.
Oh, and I promise that I'll build that museum to house our people's history. And I give you a sketch of it to take with you on your great journey to join our loved ones beyond this world eyes cannot but spirits can see.

Bertrand, holding the painting above his head and turning around in a circle so that everyone can catch a glimpse of it in the last rays of the dying sun, now places it next to Olivia.

A young girl next to the elderly woman whose hand I'm holding walks forward holding a doll. In a small but clear voice she begins:

> *As one of my most favorite people in the world,*
> *I give you this, my favorite Nanitis, to take with you and*
> *keep you company.*
> *Her eyes will help you to see in the dark, her hands will*
> *hold yours so you won't be afraid, and her shell necklace*
> *the gift to the Manitos*
> *when they greet you in the land above you now go.*
> *I'll miss you telling your stories,*
> *your voice and eyes making the creatures and people come*
> *so alive.*
> *I promise you now I'll not let them die*
> *but will tell them to other children,*
> *I hope with your voice speaking forever inside.*

She kisses the doll and lays it in the casket. Suddenly, unexpectedly, tears well up in my eyes.

Bertrand begins playing his painted drum as Oshanta joins him on a wooden flute. Still holding the hand of the older woman, I close my eyes. The drum is the sound of the earth—of beating hearts, dark colors, of longing and sadness—and the flute is the sound of the sky—of birds in flight, of light, laughter of children and no more desires.

The casket is lowered into the ground. The sun has gone down but stars are beginning to shine brightly overhead.

But Do Not, Do Not Run Away

"Fortunately, I had just finished taping my great aunt's oral accounts of the Montauk's history," Oshanta says as we sit in my living room. "It's the only oral history we have, and will be an important addition to the documentary record I'm compiling, especially since she was the last full-blooded Montaukett and the only one to still know some of the language. She also had made very careful notes of events and meetings between her and other family members over the years. Another valuable contribution is her collection, on three by five index cards, of Montauk recipes and also of herbal remedies, many handed down in writing from Samson Occum, who was thought to be the first to record such information, and her grandmother Queen Maria, who was well-known and sought after for her knowledge of local plants.

"Something we found, though, a hidden treasure no one knew about, was a number of notebooks containing children's stories she had been writing, apparently for many years. Bertrand and I remember her telling these stories to us when we were children, but we never knew they were stories she had made up. I don't know if the children at the public library in town knew either, where she was an assistant to the children's librarian and conducted story hours. However, the little girl at the funeral, a daughter of a woman who is part Montaukett and one of the children from her story hours, seemed to know. They are magical kinds of stories, based on myths that Bertrand says are a mixture of Algonquian and Iroquois, in which people transform into animals, and forces of nature are like characters in themselves—the wind, waves, sunlight. Bertrand is going to try to get them published and is thinking of doing paintings to illustrate them."

"If he has any trouble getting them published, I have a friend in New York who is an executive with a big publishing company. How is Bertrand, by the way?"

"He's working like a madman. He has a show coming up in a couple of weeks, a one-man exhibit at a prestigious gallery in the city. He's trying to complete a series of three paintings, all of my great aunt, before then. One is already done, a larger version of the one he presented at the burial. Also, he's planning to do an entire series of paintings, portraits and scenes of Montaukett life through the centuries, for the future museum. All this activity keeps him from dwelling on her death and more on fulfilling her wishes—which is what I'm trying to do, too."

She looks out the window to the ocean. "It's easier to mourn her passing in the familiar manner, to grieve over the loss, to feel this emptiness in our lives than it is to try to see death from a Native American perspective. It takes strength of imagination to fight the powerful gravity of loss, to see the dead as still living, in a kind of parallel universe to ours. This way, I believe, is also more of a tribute than the Christian way because we don't let our ancestors slip into obscurity. Their spirits are called upon to help us for generations to come, and if we have been properly appreciative, they will speak to us and guide us, as my ancestors did that day in Indian Fields. One thing we don't do is speak the deceased's name for a long time because she is traveling to that other world and we would be summoning her back to this one, confusing her spirit, if we spoke her name." Oshanta turns toward me. Around her eyes, barely perceptible lines and a faint shadow of sadness give new depth to her youthful face.

"So, I'm moving forward, full speed. After my semester law finals next week, I'm going to Washington, first to the Bureau of Indian Affairs with the letters written by the state legislators I saw in Albany. I'm also planning to do some research, to make sure I have the latest facts about the necessary steps to be declared legally a tribe. Then I'm going to meet with the new director of the Museum of Native Americans of the Smithsonian Institution about having Montauk artifacts returned to us for our museum, and about possible grants we might pursue for the building."

"An ambitious agenda. Good for you. I've been wanting to tell you I called my lawyer friend in Albany, Bob Messinger, about looking into what the State Parks Commissioner might be planning for the Montauk Park, and in particular the possibility of a golf course. He said that would be easy because environmental and historic preservation are areas he keeps a close on eye for the Governor. He got back to me the next day and said he found out that Montauk State Park is in fact listed as one of the ten sites in the park system the department is considering for development of a golf course as part of a strategy to increase revenue by appealing to what is recreationally popular. He also found out that a hydrological study was currently being prepared for the Montauk site."

"So, Marshall Kincaid and the commissioner were lying after all, hoping we'd be thrown off course thus allowing them to proceed without further hindrance. Amazing how people can look you so straight in the eye and still lie. Of course, people like the commissioner and Marshall Kincaid have been doing just that to Native Americans for a very long time." She sighs deeply. "Well, it's not as if I didn't expect it. It's just that before even taking a step forward in my fight for our land, I've first got to go backwards to fight against this."

"Yes, an unfortunate diversion. But it occurred to me, Oshanta, this fight may actually prove to be a hidden boon. The controversy could add just the impetus you need to move forward in your case. As we know, human social progress often needs a crisis to propel it forward. Most of the important advances in our justice system, like the Civil Rights laws, are the result of a controversy of some kind and proportion."

Oshanta looks into my eyes again, her face brightening. "Yes, I think you're right, Paul. So, the next step is to make the legislators aware of this water study and plan, and then put a stop to it somehow."

"If there is an overall strategy to build golf courses, it might be difficult to put a complete stop to it without well-researched reasons. A few years ago one of the client corporations of the firm I worked for in Manhattan wanted to build a new high-rise office building where a neighborhood park existed on the west side. The citizens hired an urban planning group to do a study of the neighborhood and the surrounding area. It showed a lack of 'green areas' and proved the negative impact of taking away the park. It was one of the few lawsuits we ever lost. So I would suggest asking for a plan for the entire park, which would include an assessment of its historic, archaeological and biological attributes, a description of the possible impacts a golf course would have upon them, and then an overall plan for the use of the park. In the meantime you could rally local environmental groups, such as the one that conducted the burn there, to get behind you to stop any development. And of course, gathering the Montauketts to oppose this might attract some good press, too."

"Sounds like a good plan. How do you think I should go about getting the water study to the legislators?"

"I'll get Bob to handle that. He would be someone the commissioner couldn't deny. And he'll be tactful enough so as not to sound the alarm. Better to catch them unawares so they're not prepared with a defense."

"You've been such a help, Paul." We're turned toward each other on the couch, sitting closely, and suddenly she puts her hand gently on my leg. "Sometimes I think you've been sent to me by the Great Spirit—the chance of my happening to meet someone like you here in Montauk in the winter, and precisely when all these events are beginning to unfold, really is quite incredible. But then, at other times I think I've dragged you into this when you'd rather be left alone, and you're too nice to say no."

I smile. "Well, that's quite a coincidence in itself." She looks at me quizzically. "Remember my saying you appeared in a dream I had, the dream in which you spoke the words I told you in Indian Fields the day we discovered the fire: ...*Voices of the past and of the future who fan these flames of desire and fear, threatening to consume you. You must walk through them, let them burn you if they may, but do not, do not run away?* You were a spirit in the wind telling me not to run away from understanding what had happened between my wife and me—really, understanding everything I was running away from. When I awoke, I knew that you had been sent to me. In truth, I think I knew it from the first time you came here, when you were standing right there by the window asking me if listening to the ocean had changed the way I think."

I put my arms around her now; rather than sparks and fire like the first embrace, this feels more like deeply flowing water. And Katherine's memory isn't stopping me now, as it did when I kissed Oshanta that night at her house. How long it's been since I've made love! I don't want to do anything that might spoil this moment. I hope she feels the same way, a wave coming in to meet mine. But instead I feel her strangely still, unyielding.

She looks over my shoulder and says, "I knew from what you've said you'd been in a relationship for a long time. But this is the first time you've mentioned a wife."

Suddenly struck by the fact myself, I respond, "Yes, I guess that's good. I guess that means I'm coming to terms—coming to terms with the fact that it's over. I've done a lot of thinking about my marriage since being here, but haven't wanted to accept completely that it's over. You see, we were having some problems; she had even had an affair. We separated temporarily, but I thought we'd get back together, I didn't think our problems were insurmountable until ..." This is it, these are the words! "...the day I left I found out she's going ... going to have a child by another man."

The words echo, ricocheting like bullets inside my head—*a child by another man, a child by another man.* The cry inside gets louder and louder until I can't keep it contained any longer.

Oshanta holds me tighter now. Strange, I don't feel weak or ashamed, instead a great release. And the wind spirit is here to guide me with her voice, her knowing touch. And now, *the silence between the waves, between the rising and the falling, the deep dark rumblings and shining moments.*

I see a beautiful young girl skipping toward me, her sunset hair flowing in the wind, her eyes little pieces of sky. She's laughing and singing a song: *Oh where are you father, oh where are you hiding? I'll look for you forever, all time and love abiding.* I'm inside a wooden box, but I can see her. She's close to the box now; my heart is beating so hard. She begins to open the lid but just as she does, a man comes out of thin air, grabs her and flies away with her to the sky. A doll she had been carrying and dropped lies next to me in the box.

I awake suddenly. Oshanta is next to me on the couch, my head in her lap. Oh yes, I told her about Katherine, and then must have fallen asleep.

"Were you having a dream?"

"Yes, a very strange dream." I recount it to her, every detail so real.

Excitedly, she asks, "Remember the doll the young girl gave to my great aunt? It was a Nanitis, a sacred doll the Algonquians believed to have healing powers. The dolls were kept in a box and every year at harvest time were taken out and honored with dances and feasts. They were thought to have the power to travel on their own because it was said every year when they were removed from the box their clothing and moccasins appeared worn."

Oshanta studies my face, I think wondering whether I'd mind if she ventured an interpretation. "This was a healing dream for you. The doll was a message you shouldn't despair over your loss, though you may feel dead inside now, because the beautiful girl with the sunset in her hair and sky in her eyes is not lost forever—*all time and love abiding.* But you cannot turn and hide yourself away otherwise she'll not be able to find you."

I look into Oshanta's burnt sienna earthen eyes—as beautiful, really, as sky blue eyes. I kiss her lips. We make love slowly, sweetly as the morning sun arises.

"And the Winds Would Sigh Humanely"

Journal entry, December 7:
A gray and blustery afternoon—a Montauk kind of day, as I've heard locals call such days. I understand now what Captain Lester meant by "the wind'll drive ya crazy" here. After a couple of days like this, the wind starts to sound like a mean-spirited old woman who doesn't know when everyone's heard more than enough shrill complaining, the sound screeching through the leaded windows' unseen openings and howling off the house's wood and stone. I feel pursued, driven, desperate. Then after a while, when the sound has filled up everything, it begins to seem less like something outside of my body and more like an echo inside. A gnawing hollowness and loneliness, as cold and biting as the wind, sets in.

But what about "The Dream of Fire and Wind"? We come to tear away the veil ... The wind alone unravels you filling you with fear, of the wide emptiness now you feel so near. Yes, the wind's wild energy should be used to discover something instead—a new story perhaps? Before attempting anything requiring that degree of attention, however, I need to relax. What would be perfect would be to be lying next to Oshanta by a warm glowing fire watching the light flicker over her face. But she's gone and won't be back for a few more days.

I put down my pen and journal and pick up the book next to me, *Walden*. After Thomas Berry, I want to continue on a track of nature-oriented philosophy—and who better to travel down this track with than Thoreau?

"I am no more lonely than the loon in the pond that laughs so loud, or than Walden Pond itself ... The indescribable innocence and beneficence of Nature—of sun and wind and rain, of summer and winter—such health, such cheer they afford forever! and such sympathy have they ever with our race, that all Nature would be affected, and the sun's brightness fade, and the winds would sigh humanely, and the clouds rain tears, and the woods shed their leaves and put on mourning in midsummer, if any man should ever for a just cause grieve. Shall I not have intelligence with the earth? Am I not partly leaves and vegetable mould myself?"

Such stirring, lyrical writing! As if it was the voice of Nature itself.

"Perhaps the facts most astounding and most real are never communicated by man to man. The true harvest of my daily life is somewhat as intangible as the tints of morning or evening. It is a little star-dust caught, a segment of the rainbow which I have clutched."

Breathtaking! If I could learn to write only half as well.

"Come on, Darth. The hell with the wind! Let's go for a walk—and maybe some inspiration."

As we make our way down the stairs to the beach, I spot a surfer beyond the breakers. The waves are so good he has a long and exciting ride. The surfer's fluid style and razor sharp turns on the wave's face and along its shoulder remind me of Brent, but it's impossible to recognize someone in a full dry suit, especially from this distance. We walk to where he's starting to come in.

"Brent, is that you?"

"Hey, man. How've you been?"

"Okay. At first I was a little envious of you out there, but once I felt the water, the envy quickly disappeared. The wind is a bit brutal, too."

"Yeah, it's pretty cold. Your face gets numb to it after a while. And the wind is tough, but the waves are so fine, I couldn't resist."

"Will you be going out much longer?"

"Maybe one or two more times. Then I'll be heading to Vermont for the winter, teaching snowboarding at Killington."

"Seems like a good arrangement—Montauk in the summer and Vermont in the winter."

"Yeah, it is, but next year I'm going to Australia. I love Montauk, but I need a change of scenery."

"New waves to conquer."

"Definitely."

"Would you like to come up to the house to warm up a bit?"

"Sure, man. That would be great." As we walk up the stairs, I see someone waving to me at the top.

"Bertrand, what a surprise! Good to see you. This is Brent, my eminently skillful surfing instructor."

"Nice to meet you, Brent."

"Bertrand's a painter. How's the work going?"

He smiles broadly. "I've just finished my paintings for the show. I need to unwind, and reward myself somehow. So, I've come to ask if you'd like to join me in a ceremony. I've been secretly working on building a sweat lodge, similar to one that was built in the Pharaoh Village many years ago. I want to initiate it, and I'd like you to join me. You're welcome to come too if you want, Brent. If you're a friend of Paul's you're a friend of mine."

"Well, yes. It's an honor, Bertrand. Besides the fact it's probably just the thing one needs on a day like this."

"I'd be psyched, man. Definitely just what I need."

We drive to Bertrand's house and follow him into a small wooded area on the north side.

"Someday, when the land becomes ours again, I'll build one in the Pharaoh Village, though I could actually just move this one there. Sweat lodges were traditionally made to be easily taken down and moved."

We come to a small rounded hut covered with pieces of bark.

"I feel as if I've suddenly traveled back hundreds of years in time."

"Yeah, this is really cool. You built it with materials from around here?" Brent asks.

"Yes. The bark sheets are from oak trees, the matting underneath are phragmites reeds tied together, and the branches forming the frame inside are made from red cedar saplings. My grandmother told me that chestnut was traditionally used by my ancestors for the bark, because it was sturdier and more weather-resistant than oak, but chestnut trees are almost nonexistent here now. Red maple and black locust were also used for the saplings in the past, but I chose the red cedar for its aromatic smell, though there is less of it than red maple. The matting used to be made of cattails, but they are scarce now, too.

"There were apparently a number of different kinds of sweat lodges built by the Algonquians—some made of clay and reeds, others of clay and earth. This one is basically the same construction as their wigwams were, except for not having an opening in the middle for smoke from a fire to escape. I wanted to see if I could build one.

"So, shall we, gentlemen? Everything is ready for us inside."

We enter through a reed doorway covered with a length of leather hide. Inside it's very warm, like a sauna. The room is a little over six feet high in the center, the only part we can stand up in without hunching over, and is maybe 20 feet around. The floor is covered with reed matting and scattered swatches of what look to be deerskins. There's a wooden bench and two small tables, one with a few towels folded upon it and another with a teapot and some cups. In the center of the room is a pile of hot stones upon a screen, under which are burning embers in a small pit in the earth. Near it are a large clay pot and another smaller pot.

"Now, please take a towel and seat yourselves wherever you'd like. Then I'll bring you a cup of horsemint tea that helps induce a good sweat. You'll probably want to take off your clothes."

Bertrand takes a large cup from the small pot, scoops dirt from it and pours it onto the embers. He then removes his clothes, takes a towel and drapes it around his neck. After pouring the tea, he dunks the pitcher into the large clay pot and tosses water onto the hot stones until the room is sufficiently steamy, which doesn't take long, given the room's hobbit-like size. Brent and I take our clothes off too.

Breathing in the steam, I feel all the tightness in my muscles begin to disappear. I throw back my head and turn my neck from side to side. Through the clouds of steam I can still see the inside of the lodge. How evenly and carefully the thatching is tied, and the horizontal and vertical saplings underneath it. Not a breath of steam seems to be escaping, and what wonderful smells are coming alive in the steaminess: the salt marsh smell from the reeds, a piney freshness from the cedar saplings, the earthy muskiness of the deerskins, and cool cleansing aroma of the horsemint tea.

"This is proof engineering and design need not be sophisticated to be efficient, and that it can be beautiful as well as functional. What a different feeling sitting in here is compared to the white tiled steam room at the club I belong to in the City. I feel I'm not only getting a steam, but that I'm getting healed in some other way."

"The Algonquians believed that sitting in the sweat lodge could cure just about anything ailing one's body, mind or spirit. They believed the spirit residing in the stone is awakened by the heat of the fire. The spirit steam created when water is sprinkled upon the rocks enters the body and drives out everything causing one pain. Thus, before the Manito returns to the stone it has imparted some of its nature to the body, which is why one feels so well after being in a sweat lodge."

I recall the experience with Oshanta when we came upon the rock in the woods and the poem she recited: *"I am hard and my surface cold... within these hard edges many stories I hold of the great creatures who in these woods dwelled and now are no more ... but I always have hope for, every now and then, someone will touch me and hear me among Men."*

"I'm sure there are people who'd prefer the white-tiled steam room to this, maybe they'd even be afraid of being in here, like the way I've found some people to be afraid of swimming in the ocean."

"Maybe at first, Brent," Bertrand says. "But I think there are some things humans will respond to, because they're rooted somewhere in a deep recess of our brain, even if long-buried beneath white tiles and steel skyscrapers—like wood, these reeds, like fire, sunsets and oceans."

"'Shall I not have intelligence with the earth? Am I not partly leaves and vegetable mould myself?' A line from *Walden* I was reading this morning," I offer.

"That's really cool. I know I feel like I'm part of the ocean, more like a fish sometimes. It sounds strange, but the ocean feels kind of like my home. I think I ran away to the sea to drown out the sounds—of the yelling, the hitting, the crying in my house, and almost worse, the silence afterwards, my mother's silence."

Brent breathes deeply in and out. "That's why I love to teach surfing. I believe it can save your life. And it teaches you true respect and humility, not the screwed up kind you can get from your family."

Through the clouds of steam I see him look up, the beginning of a smile on his face, his eyes shining a dark ocean blue. "My dream is someday to start an organization that will help kids from abusive families, introduce them to the ocean."

"That's a noble goal, Brent. I think you're right that nature can save one's life. When you feel you don't belong to anything or anyone, cast adrift in a lonely world, it's the one thing that gives you a sense of belonging, of being rooted somewhere. Something calls you, comforts you, like an ancient long-lost song in your soul."

Bertrand's words harken back to something familiar—yes, the night I came out here and was standing on the bluffs, the ocean's waves calling me back to some long-lost place of my youth, of walks in the woods, the sense of adventure, of newness and excitement I found there. Are the mythic pictures we form of the places we inhabited most profoundly in our pasts the sources of our most powerful dreams and hopes and imaginings? Like modern Odysseuses all, do we wander through this world of labyrinthine freeways, neon skies and numbing shopping malls forever seeking to return to a shining, lyrical place that is our true and only home? But is there really such a place, or is it just the fantasy that keeps us searching, faithfully slaying everyday demons in our way, in hopes we'll find our way back someday?

I peer through the vaporous air for a passing glimpse of Bertrand's face. It's one of the most animated faces I've ever known: his blue-green eyes can flash with bolts of anger no less fiery than their rays of generosity; his broad smile can surround you in its happiness just as his scowl can make you feel his anger. But at this moment, his face appears strangely peaceful. Brent, who usually has a compulsive cheerfulness about his face, as if he were keeping a bubbling chaos under control just beneath the surface, is also radiating calmness now. No demons in their way; no trying to be anything or anywhere else.

"But to be able to carry in your mind that sunset, that wave or smell of the earth, so their poetry is always speaking to you, no matter where you are, is the secret. Then you'll feel no separateness. Only the moment as the wind blows by your cheek and the bird flies overhead."

As Bertrand says these last words, I finally feel the last tightness in my body—around my mouth and across my forehead—disappear. Once in a great while, "the facts most astounding and most real" *can* be "communicated by man to man ... a little star-dust caught, a segment of the rainbow which I have clutched."

"Well, there's only one thing to do now, to put the icing on the cake, so to speak: a quick, invigorating jump in the sea. It's what my ancestors would do after being in the sweat lodge. It balances the body and closes the skin's pores."

Brent and I exchange a questioning look through the thinning veil of steam.

"Trust me, it won't feel that cold, because your body is very warm now, and the harbor is only about 200 feet east through the woods."

"Okay. I'm up for it."

"Lead the way, fearless leader."

Like Bertrand, we put on only our shoes and tie a towel around our waist, carrying our clothes.

Darth, who's been sitting patiently outside, follows behind Bertrand, his excitement mounting as we near the harbor. Quickly shedding shoes and towels, we run for the water. As we plunge in, our laughs ripple across the icy water ... *I am no more lonely than the loon in the pond that laughs so loud.* As I emerge above the surface, a sudden wind blows by my cheek ... *and the winds would sigh humanely ...*

Still, Still that Clamorous Churning

"Listen to this: 'Golf Course Planned for Indian Lands—New York State Assemblyman Fred Connor has announced his opposition to the Office of Parks, Recreation and Historic Preservation's proposal for a golf course on land where the Montauk Indians once dwelled.' Your friend in Albany sure works fast. I didn't expect an article in *Newsday* to greet me when I got back. Connor is asking for a Master Plan with a full environmental study of the area and a moratorium on any work until it is completed. Apparently, Kincaid's company, Out East Development, was awarded a contract for the project over three months ago, pending the results of the hydrology study."

"Does it mention any of the study's findings?"

"It says engineers found there wasn't enough water in the area, but Park Commissioner Robert Rank proposes a link-up with the public water system to solve that problem. He's also quoted, as follows: 'I believe this is a sound plan. We have balanced environmental, historic and recreational needs on this site. We have done our homework. Everyone can end up a winner in this. And I look forward to the opportunity to show everyone how at the public meeting Assemblyman Connor has suggested.'"

"Is there a date set for a meeting yet?"

"Yes, next week at East Hampton Town Hall."

"The possibility of obtaining public water for the golf course is certainly disappointing news. Inadequate water was one of the strongest environmental arguments."

"Yes, and I'm afraid they'll argue that carving 150 acres—that's what I found out 18-hole golf courses require, though maybe they'll want 300 acres for 36 holes—out of the park's 1500 is not such a big deal, and besides, the land they'd use is mostly mere scrub and brush land. And, what's more, most of it has already been cleared by fire. How convenient. And then maybe the rare grasses can be isolated to the satisfaction of the Conservation Society and with public water being used and perhaps few fertilizers, environmental groups might be quieted—in which case our best argument will be from the archaeological and historical side.

"I'll get Samson to speak—he's the best-known among us in the community and a good orator, as you know—and Bertrand and I will speak."

"And try to fill the room with as many Montauketts as you can. So, how did you make out in Washington?"

"Very well. The official I met with at the Bureau of Indian Affairs gave me encouraging news regarding federal recognition. It's not as difficult a process as it used to be. Thankfully, there's no more having to prove how much of a Montaukett one is through blood, so we'll show how present-day Montauks connect back to Wyandanch through records of genealogies. Then, we'll prove that we've had tribal governments and meetings as a group over time.

"As to our land claim based on historic deeds, he thought we had a sound case there, too. I also presented Assemblyman Connor's and our state senator's letters supporting our efforts to establish ourselves as a tribe."

"What about the congressman from this district? Have you contacted him?"

"I tried to speak to him when I was in Washington, but he was unavailable. I did speak to an aide who said she would have him call me. One other important contact I made was with a lawyer from the Native American Trust, an organization dedicated to helping provide legal aid to tribes seeking to regain their ancestral lands."

"Good work. I think you said in between all this work in Washington you were going to take your law finals. How did that go?"

The Last Resort

"I think I did well. I spoke to one of my professors who said I could take more credits next semester—an honors class—so I can finish in a year from now rather than a year and a half."

"That's great. I guess that means you'll be spending more time in the City beginning in a month or so."

"Yes. But I'll try to come out every weekend." She studies my face. "What about your plans, Paul? Will you be going back to the City soon?" she asks gently.

"To tell you the truth, I really haven't thought about it. Hopefully, I'll know the right thing to do when the time comes to decide." I look out her window across the still, quiet harbor.

"Did you hear that?" Oshanta asks.

"No, I didn't hear anything."

"It sounded like someone knocked on the side of the house."

We walk outside into the late afternoon. No one is at the front door. Oshanta walks down the steps around to the side. I follow her. There, sticking out of the wall is an arrow. We turn to each other in disbelief.

"Let's call the police right away. Is it at all possible it was from a hunter? Is it deer hunting season now?"

"I'm not sure," Oshanta says in a shaky voice. "Maybe. But it would be a bizarre coincidence, don't you think? An arrow shot into the side of an Indian's house?"

"I'd say it's probably a hunter's arrow gone really astray," the officer says as he shines the flashlight on the arrow and pulls it out with his gloved hand. "It does happen to be bow hunting season for deer. Strange part is closest legal deer hunting property is clear across the harbor. Course, we do get poachers from time to time. Especially in recent years, with the deer population multiplying like it is. And in these woods here with few people around 'mam, it's probably a prime spot for poachers."

"I've never encountered any deer hunters before here, officer, and my great aunt, who lived next door for 90 years, never mentioned any hunting here either."

"Well, I'll take it in and get it to the crime lab, see if we can identify any fingerprints. I wouldn't be too worried though."

"Please let me know as soon as you find out anything, officer."

"Maybe he should take the note you received a few weeks ago, Oshanta. See if there are any fingerprints that might match up."

"Now that you mention it, I noticed an envelope in my mail today that reminded me of the one that note came in." We walk into the house. Oshanta finds the note in a desk draw. Looking closely at the envelope, she leafs hurriedly through some unopened mail on top of her desk, picks out one letter and opens it.

"'Don't make a scene, if you know what I mean. Let the future take its course then no reason for force.'"

But I Could Hear the Cries

As I approach the Town Hall, six Native Americans dressed in traditional costumes are marching in front with signs saying "After 300 Years of Injustice, Instead of Apologies we get Par Threes" and "No to White Men with Golf Balls on our Ancient Montauk Soils." A television cameraman is filming them, and Bertrand is on the lawn playing his drum. I smile and wave to him.

Inside, the meeting room is quite crowded. Another television cameraman is positioning himself along the side. I spot Oshanta toward the front, sitting next to Samson.

"I'm glad to see the natives are restless."

"Paul, I'm glad you came. I saved a seat for you."

"Certainly appears to be a good turn-out."

"Yes, I just hope most of them are on our side," Oshanta says as she looks around nervously. "But one thing is for sure: no one can say the Montauks don't exist."

"How many are here?"

"I think 50. There are 25 from Montauk, Sag Harbor and East Hampton, 20 from the rest of the Island and five came all the way from Wisconsin."

"I only know two people in this area outside of you, Bertrand and Samson, and my surfing instructor is the one I knew how to get in touch with, so I asked him to come. He, Bertrand and I spent a memorable afternoon recently in a sweat lodge. He also saved my life. There he is coming in now." I stand up and wave to him.

"Brent, I'd like you to meet Oshanta, Bertrand's cousin. And this is Reverend Samson Occum, another cousin of Bertrand's."

"Glad to meet you both. I saw Bertrand out front playing the drum. Very cool. Gets you in the right spirit."

"If you plan to say anything, Brent, you have to sign up in front."

"I haven't had much practice at public speaking, but I do want to say a few words."

As Brent walks forward, I whisper to Oshanta, "Any word from the police department yet?"

"The fingerprints didn't match anything they had, which is what I expected would be the case, though I'd heard rumors that Kincaid had been arrested when he was a kid for stealing a car, so I was hopeful there would be something to turn up. The prints on the paper and the arrow did match up. I imagine I hear arrows being shot into my house and have nightmares about Marshall Kincaid. That's him sitting next to the commissioner in the front row. Even looking at him from the back sends a bit of a chill up my spine."

"Have you told Samson or Bertrand?"

"No, I don't want to alarm them, or for them to think they need to protect me."

"This meeting will now come to order. For those of you who don't know, I'm State Assemblyman Fred Connor. We're here to present our views on an important matter to the local citizenry, especially from Montauk, regarding proposed development of State Park land in Montauk into a golf course. Everyone who has requested to speak will have the opportunity, and I'll call you up to the podium in the order in which you signed up.

"But first, New York State Commissioner of Parks, Recreation and Historic Preservation, Mr. Robert Rank, will tell us about what his department has proposed. After everyone has had a chance to speak, I'll make my comments."

The commissioner, his dark blue suit pulling around the middle, marches confidently up to the podium. Next to it a large map is displayed on an easel.

Smiling for the cameras, he begins. "Glad to see so many of you good citizens here today, and glad to have this opportunity to tell you about the exciting plans we have for Montauk. And I mean exciting, because rarely does the department have the chance to provide one plan that truly fulfills the goals of each facet of our mission: conservation, recreation and historic preservation.

"Now," he takes the pointer and directs it at the map, a close-up of the park, "of the park's 1500 acres, only 200 are actually used now by the public: 50 acres along the Block Island Sound beach side for fishing and swimming and 150 for hiking and fishing around Big Reed Pond. Most of the park's 1300 remaining acres have been inaccessible, covered with mostly non-native brush and vines that have grown up in the last 100 years or so, since it was used as pastureland. With the help of the Conservation Society, we have recently conducted a controlled burn of about 200 acres in this area south of Big Reed to cut back this growth which has impeded the growth of native grasses and plants which the Conservation Society and we would like to revive.

"Now, north of Big Reed there's a sand and marsh area behind the dunes, covering about 150 acres. What we'd like to do is use about 100 acres here and the 200 acres where we've burned and create one of the most beautiful and unusual championship golf courses on the entire east coast. Because what we want to do is set aside all of the special plant and geological features of the land—the dunes, the native grasses, the marshes and bogs—and build the course around them. Nothing of significance will be disturbed.

"As far as the historic aspect in all this, we plan to designate the Montauk Indian Village which is here, comprising about 20 acres just south of Big Reed, a historic site. In addition, we're setting aside money to continue archaeological excavations in this area, and for the Montauks to develop a museum with their artifacts which would be located here, at the entrance to the nature trails and the trails to the village. Next to the museum, we also have planned a nature study center for various groups, like the Conservation Society, to use for environmental educational purposes.

"The last historic element of the plan is to restore the office building and the barn at the southern entrance to the park. This 200 year-old building will remain the park office but also become a club house, and the barn will become the maintenance shed. Great care will be taken to maintain architectural integrity.

"So, you can see that we've taken everyone's needs into consideration here—the environmental community, the Native Americans, the history buffs, the recreational community and the business community. Of all the outdoor recreational groups that our state parks accommodate—hikers, bikers, swimmers, fishing enthusiasts and golfers—none is growing as fast as golfers. And Montauk needs another public golf course. The County course is so crowded people wait for hours to get on.

"With the help of the Conservation Society, we'll be completing an environmental assessment of the park and then a Master Plan, which is long overdue, along with detailed maps of every aspect of the plan in the coming months. We won't be using fertilizers or pesticides on this course—it'll be like the naturalistic links courses in Scotland—but we'll still need to water the greens some, though only when it gets very dry in the middle of the summer. The water study we conducted proved there was not enough groundwater in the area, as we suspected. So, we'll be using public water supplied through a hook-up with the County pipeline in Napeague.

"We welcome any suggestions the community may have toward the success of the plan, which we hope to begin implementing by April of next year. Thank you for your time."

Obviously pleased with himself, he smiles even more broadly and puffs himself out a bit, causing the button that had been straining on his jacket to pop off. But the sound is lost in the applause from a sizable portion of the audience.

"Pretty smooth character when he wants to be," I whisper to Oshanta.

"Yes, I was afraid he'd make it sound attractive, not only to business people and golfers but even to the likes of the Conservation Society, which he apparently already has onboard. And that's why the director told me she wouldn't be commenting on the plan at this point."

"The next speaker will be Reverend Samson Occum." In his long, dignified gait, Samson strides to the podium. As preachers do from a pulpit before beginning a sermon, he slowly surveys the flock, gathering in each one with his benevolent, fatherly gaze.

"What we've heard, good people, is not an inherently bad plan. As a matter of fact, I have to agree with the commissioner that it does take every interest group into consideration, and on its face appears to be balanced and equitable. However, one must look farther back, back into a sorrowful and unjust past, to judge whether 20 acres arbitrarily set aside for archaeological study of a Montaukett village in this area is enough. How can it be determined that 20 acres is sufficient before study has determined it as such?

"Speaking as a Montaukett, I appreciate the gesture for the funds for a museum, which is something we have wanted to build. But we also would like to build a school on this land.

"So, while it is not a bad plan, as a Montaukett I cannot accept it. This was land we once lived on for centuries, taken from us by broken and devious deeds. We've not been treated justly by governments in the past. We hope *that* time has ended at long last and governments and their leaders will redeem themselves in the eyes of God and everyone and finally make amends. And to this hope, I'll conclude with words from a hymn my forefather Reverend Samson Occum composed the same year white settlers proclaimed their independence from their oppressors in England, in1776:

*When to the law I trembling fled, it poured its curses upon
my head. I no relief could find;
This fearful truth increased my pain ...
But while I thus in anguish lay, the gracious Saviour
passed this way ... The sinner, by His justice slain, now by
His grace is born again,
and sings redeeming love.*

Everyone sits quietly at first, mesmerized by the resonant power of his voice, his words, his presence. Then most of the audience begins applauding, reverently it seems, even some who had applauded for the commissioner, whether they agreed with Samson's message or not.

"Now we'll hear from Captain Harold Lester."

"I know him," I whisper to Oshanta. "He helped me catch my Thanksgiving striped bass. He also helped Brent save my life."

In his stained, long-billed fishing hat, rubber boots and canvas pants held up with faded red suspenders and smelling strongly of fish and the sea, Captain Lester begins.

"My name is Capem' Harold Lester. I live in Accabonac as my family has for 300 years, back to the beginning when the first boatload of us from the northern shores of England landed on this fair, forgiving land. Down through the years, stories got passed on. Not a lot survive today, but one that does is how the Montauketts showed the first Lesters and Bennetts their favorite places to fish and dig for oysters, clams and scallops. Saved those ol' Bonackers' lives, they did. Now, where your best places are is not somethin' most fishermen would ever share with anybody that wasn't at least kin, and even then a lot just don't let on. These are secrets guarded with your life.

"So, that's one of the reasons, a sorta thank-you, I'm here to speak for the Indians rights to that land in Montauk where you want to build this golf course. The other is cuz of a kinda kinship feelin with 'em because of our pasts. Course God and everyone know they certainly got pushed 'round more than us. But the government takin' away our fishing rights as ocean haulseiners is not much different than takin' away their rights to the land they lived on, hunted and grew crops on for generations. What the ocean is to us Bonac baymen, the land is to them, as I see it. Yep. Same story. New folk, like the sport fishermen in their fancy boats and the golfers, come and they couldn't give a damn 'bout us. We just in their way. So we gotta speak out. We been fightin' for our rights in Albany for years now. Indians been fightin' for theirs for 300, and they still fightin'. High time we do the right thing by them, as the good Reverend says. That's all I got to say today."

As he walks awkwardly from the podium, as if he really was made more for the sea than the land, his reddish complexion becomes even redder with sudden self-consciousness and surprise from the enthusiastic applause of many in the crowd and the cameras focusing in on him. I wave to him as he passes by. Oshanta's name is called. Perhaps taking a cue from Samson, she surveys the crowd before beginning to speak, looking the commissioner and Marshall Kincaid squarely in the eye. I see her put something on the podium, which looks like a stone. It must be the thunderbird stone her great aunt had given her—"the thunder of his wings and fire of his eyes to help you in your battles, and his wisdom as your guide."

"I will not go on at length, for my cousin Reverend Occum and the gentleman who preceded me both expressed much of my own sentiment. I'll add that having our land in Indian Fields, which comprises all of the land where the commissioner is proposing his plan, returned to the Montauk tribe is not a pipe dream. I recently was in Washington speaking to officials at the Bureau of Indian Affairs and was given encouraging news. I also made contact with a group that assists Native Americans with their land claims, though I will be the lead counsel in this claim, when I receive my law degree a year from now.

"There are other courses for golfers to golf on, and other places to build new ones. There are not other lands the Montauks can claim as their ancestral land which aren't already occupied by houses and other development. I think an environmental center and a Montauk Indian Museum are appropriate uses for Indian Fields. But to say the land must be used defeats part of the purpose of preserving land, and the reason the State, in its wisdom, saved this land from the bulldozer to begin with.

"I look forward to the findings of the environmental impact statement to assess all the features of this land. I'm confident the archaeological description will reveal, as Reverend Occum suggested, that 20 acres is hardly the extent of the sensitive land.

"I thank Assemblyman Connor for bringing this issue into the open for all to see and comment upon, and to all of you who have come here today. And to the Commissioner and Out East Development, I say the past will never stay at rest as long as there are those who force their profit-filled futures upon that past. And the inheritors of that past will not fear clever slings or arrows."

As she sits down, I whisper, "That was very impressive. And I liked the allusion at the end. As I've said before, you're going to make a terrific lawyer—calm and factual, with the right amount of fire and thunder to get peoples' attention." She smiles and squeezes my hand.

Marshall Kincaid approaches the podium. He looks flustered and angry. But, like a chameleon, or as Oshanta prefers to call him, the Trickster, he suddenly displays a smiling affability, the good guy next door.

"Most of you in here know me. I've built some of your homes and businesses and others may know me from the local organizations I like to support. You know I wouldn't want to build something in this community that wasn't quality, and wasn't something that people want and need. That's because I take a lot of pride in being part of this great place my forefathers lived in for 200 years. Not as long as the Montauk Indians, I grant you, but long enough to care a lot.

"I've been watching that barn and house at the park, where my grandfather was born, deteriorate over the years. And it breaks my heart. I know the State doesn't have the money to spend. So, I'm willing to pay for it, out of my own pocket. As far as the golf course, it's something a lot of people want. And it'll be affordable to the average person, to local people, not rich second-home owners like those who belong to the Maidstone or the other private clubs.

"The local schools can use the nature center for outdoor education studies and the Montauk Indian Museum for its history studies. There's something for everyone in this plan, as the commissioner said. Yes, we've got to honor the past and preserve it, but we've also got to look to the future. And I promise you, this plan will do both. Thank you all for coming."

"The Wily Coyote gave a pretty clever speech," I say to Oshanta amid the clapping.

"Bertrand Pharaoh."

Bertrand had been standing in the back near the entrance. Dressed in jeans and a deerskin jacket with painted animals upon it—deer, wolves, birds and fish—and carrying his drum, he walks up the aisle with that stride of god-like composure and grace I remember when he walked out of the water the day I met him. As Samson's presence is commanding in a somber way, Bertrand's is in a radiant way. Light just seems to emanate from him, his blue-green eyes, his light golden brown skin, even his black hair—perhaps the way in which Olivia said light shone from Stephen Pharaoh.

"I'm going to tell a story my grandmother used to tell. Once there was a turtle named Tom who lived happily in the woods and ponds where many generations of turtles had lived before. They worked hard, provided for their young and generally got on quite well with their neighbors, the fox, the rabbit and the deer. The one rule was not to go out beyond a certain row of trees, because there were coyotes out there that seemed very nice and you'd want to take one home to meet your family, but on the way back, they could change into something called a man. When you arrived home, the man would put you and all the other turtles in little boxes with little dishes of water and food and then take your turtle land.

"But Tom was a curious turtle, so he ventured out beyond the certain row of trees and soon found himself face to face with a coyote. "Oh little turtle, how cute you are. Why don't you take me to meet your family?" So, believing the coyote to be quite nice, Tom brought the coyote home. And sure enough, the coyote had become a man and put all the turtles in boxes and then built houses and stores on the land. But Tom the turtle and a few others escaped the man's hand. And they went to the court where all the creatures and men could discuss their disagreements in a civilized way. They told of what happened to their family and relatives, but the judge of the court did not seem to care. They went back again and again, when finally a judge said yes, they could have their land back, it was only fair, and all the turtles would be released from their boxes and returned to their land. But when they returned, they found most of it covered with buildings and roads. There was one section, however, that was spared. A grove of trees and a small pond, and this is where the turtles lived once again.

"So, that's really it. Out of the 10,000 acres the Montauks once inhabited on this peninsula, the 1500 acres in the State Park is all that's left unspoiled we could return to, and we would probably want for ourselves only about 300 of those acres around the Pharaoh Village site. There is Hither Woods, of course, which is an even larger piece of preserved land, but Indian Fields is where most of our ancestors dwelled, so that is where we should go. We're not asking very much. Just to leave it alone until we prove it to be legally ours in the courts. Thank you." As he walks down the aisle and the cameras zoom in, he beats his drum in a quick, dramatic flourish.

"Paul Collins has requested to speak next."

"I have lived in Montauk only a very short time, but in that time I've become acquainted with a few members of the Montauk tribe and with their story. As a lawyer, not to mention as a white American, I believe injustice has been done to these people through the centuries and that they have a legitimate legal case on their hands, from what I know so far. And I plan to know more, for I'll be helping them in their case. It would be a shame if the State spent millions of dollars on a golf course that might simply be torn up in the end, if the Montauks win their case. So, my advice is to hold off, at least for a year, to see what comes of their efforts. Thank you."

Oshanta grabs my hand as I sit down. "I didn't know you were joining my legal team, counselor."

"I only decided this morning. I hope you approve. When you mentioned the Native American Trust, I looked into it and there's an office in Manhattan. I'm hoping to arrange things so I can still live out here part of the time. I'll have to familiarize myself with the laws and case law, but I figure if I can successfully defend a corporation's turf in the market place, I can probably defend Native Americans turf in the real world—and it will certainly be a whole lot more satisfying." She looks like she wants to kiss me.

"Lucille Edwards, Executive Director of the Chamber of Commerce."

A well-groomed woman of about 50 approaches the podium. Reading from a prepared statement, she begins speaking.

"The Board of Directors of the Montauk and East Hampton Chambers of Commerce are unanimously in support of the State Park's plan for a golf course. We think it will benefit, not only businesses relating to tourism, such as restaurants and motels, but also the community as a whole recreationally. We conducted an informal survey about a year ago, asking local people what they'd like to see here in terms of development, and most said a golf course. We think this is a very balanced plan and should move forward without hindrance."

Removing her rectangular reading glasses, she looks up from her paper with a severe, self-righteous look on her face. "There's only one thing I'd like to add to our formal statement. In the light of so much apparent support for the Indians, my concern is whether they might want to put a gambling casino on that property. Everyone knows how popular the casino on the Indian reservation in Connecticut is, and how much money it makes for them. Now, that would be a kind of commerce that we wouldn't like to see here. Thank you."

Oshanta, Samson, Brent and I exchange surprised glances.

"Our last speaker will be Brent Osborne."

With his hands stuffed in his baggy pants and trying hard not to look down and hide behind the blond hair falling across his face, Brent begins.

"I'm a surfer, and I don't know a lot about the Montauk Indians' history. But recently I had a chance to spend some time with one of the speakers here today, Bertrand Pharaoh, and I know he's committed to preserving that land the way it is and to preserving something of his peoples' way of life, not to putting any casino on it for gambling. That's not how he thinks, and I'm sure that's not how the Reverend thinks either." Pausing for a second, thinking hard about what he wants to say, Brent is gaining in confidence now, his deep ocean-blue eyes looking out at the audience, sparkling like sunlight reflected on water.

"Bertrand understands that nature can make us feel a freedom we can't feel anywhere else. I've been coming out here a long time to surf, and it's really getting built up. Soon the reason people come here will be gone. That sense of freedom, beauty and peace you find in nature is that reason, even if people aren't aware it is. Some might say, well, a golf course is beautiful and peaceful and it's nature. But it isn't. It's manmade nature, which isn't even close to the same thing. I guess that's it."

"Your friend was terrific. He ended everything on just the right note," Oshanta says as we applaud.

"I think we all benefited from this forum," Assemblyman Connor says. "I'll look forward to the environmental assessment and Master Plan of the park, and carefully weigh all the merits and disadvantages to the plan at that time. Copies of the plan will be made available to the public and a public hearing will be held. Thank you everyone for your time and your words."

As we arise, the commissioner and Marshall Kincaid hurry over to us.

"Ah, Miss Pharaoh? Well, we appreciated your comments."

"Did you really, commissioner? That's a surprise."

"We want to work with you and your people. I was just thinking, what would you say about 50 acres instead of 20? And maybe a bigger museum, with an extra room for a classroom?"

Oshanta seems so amazed by this absurd, offensive pandering that she bursts out laughing. Their grinning though transparent amiability rapidly evaporates. "Just as in the story of the turtle and the coyote, you want to put us in neat tiny boxes, pacify us with small offerings of food and water. You actually think you're being generous, too. That's what's amazing. Well, I guess in terms of how you think and how you do things—which is getting what you want, no matter what—then you are being generous, in which case I'll say thank you, but no thank you."

They scowl hard at her, Kincaid even more intensely, shooting sharp arrows with his eyes.

"They obviously think you've won this round," I say as we leave the building.

"I suppose, though it doesn't mean much in the end. The commissioner says he's interested in the public's comments, but he's really not. He'll only consider those comments that further the "success" of his plan. In his mind it's a done deal. The way he throws these numbers around—20 acres here, 50 there—also makes me worry that the environmental impact statement won't be as objective as it should be which is the only hope we have to fight this thing. Is it possible the Department of Parks could influence how the Department of Environmental Conservation will review it?"

"I guess anything is possible in politics. But I'll make sure my friend Bob Messinger keeps his eye on things for us. And Assemblyman Connors appears he'll be objective. Then we'll have the public hearing to make comments. I'll tell you who worries me—Marshall Kincaid. That look he just gave you was so spiteful, an out-to-get-you look if I've ever seen one. I've never seen anyone transform so quickly from Mr. Nice Guy to Mr. Mean."

"A classic coyote complex is my diagnosis." We both laugh.

"But didn't you say the classic coyote sees some light in the end, redeems himself in some way?"

"Maybe that *is* simply a myth. Like Samson's hopeful words from Christian symbols, they're ennobling only to the few they speak to, not to the many like Marshall Kincaid and Commissioner Rank who only hear their own words and the omnipotent sound of money."

"You're beginning to sound as bleak about humanity as Bertrand."

"Maybe I need to be—part of the wisdom of the Thunderbird I need for my battle. Remember the words of my great aunt about the lesson of the fire: one needs to see a thing's opposite in order to see it clearly. Pure idealism is fine in art, religion and philosophy, but it doesn't seem to work well in dealing with people."

Snow Falling on the Ocean

Journal entry, December 20:
Looking back to my first entry in this journal almost two months ago, on the day after landing in Montauk, I wondered if I could create a new life for myself, "as a novelist creates a character in a book ... just be no one for a while, choose no particular life until what life I want becomes clear." The dream I had of running aground on a raft, wanting to walk into the sea and the waves swallow me up; then came the voice from the woods, calling.

Now there's Oshanta and new legal work that's rekindled a fire for my profession I haven't felt since starting out so many years ago. I'll also be here three days a week to pursue whatever else I wish—write poetry, surf and walk on the beach with Darth.

Like the blade of grass I saw in the dunes my first day here, I let the wind blow me, bend me, to create new lines upon the sand.

I think I'm even able to face Katherine now, to sign the papers, to say goodbye.

I look up from my journal. Snow is falling on the ocean, its whiteness sadly beautiful against the somber gray of sea and sky. I pick up my pen again.

How still and hushed the water seems, the way the land becomes when it snows, wrapping the world in a soft, protective cover of white. Yet the delicate crystalline designs from far reaches of the sky disappear as they meet with the wide dark sea—perhaps an apt metaphor for how the good can dissolve as it encounters the ocean of dark human motives; the way, as Oshanta said, our noblest ideals can seem to exist in a separate realm—in the fiction of art and religious beliefs, the words of Thomas Berry and Thoreau.

How we want so to believe that moments of fineness and calm will last forever, how good fortune won't disappear.

So moments like this, of crystalline designs falling fortuitously from the sky into a peaceful sea, we must hold in our minds, making them into something new, something that will last forever.

Acknowledgments

First, I'd like to acknowledge the encouragement to write from my English teacher at Northampton School for Girls, Mrs. Cantarella. She was a fearsome figure, and her voice admonishing me to "pay attention" and maybe I could be a good writer still echoes in my mind today. Though I never did end up working with him, the praise of literary agent Peter Shepard of Harold Ober Associates was an important impetus years ago for me to continue working at writing a good novel. I'd like to thank my writer friend Celine Keating who offered early and unflagging support for this novel, and to my cousin Dr. Jim I. Jones, who, though on the nerdy scientific side, liked this novel from the beginning and encouraged me to find a publisher. I much appreciate the support of Stephanie Krusa and the other folks at the Third House Nature Center. Lastly, I'd like to thank my publisher, Pam Knight, who helped make this book better and has brought it finally into the light of day.

About the Author

Photo by Kris Christine

Kay Tobler Liss is a writer and editor, having worked for newspapers and magazines in New York and Maine for many decades. Among the magazines she worked for were *Sunstorm Arts*, *House* and *Hamptons Magazine,* and was managing editor of *The Shelter Island Reporter*. She studied literature at Bard College and Environmental Studies at Southampton College and has taught courses in both fields in New York and Maine. She won a prize for her poetry at 17 years old, and was published in the Smith College literary magazine. She lived in Montauk, N.Y. for 13 years and now lives in Maine. This is her first novel.

CPSIA information can be obtained
at www.ICGtesting.com
Printed in the USA
LVHW021727160720
660875LV00015B/1646